Sita's

Raghav Khanna comes from the world of films and television where he has donned many hats—writer, director, producer and a studio executive. He is best known as the creative director and writer of the acclaimed food history series *Raja Rasoi aur Anya Kahaniyaan*.

His other notable works include *Masters of Taste, The Family Affair, Mega-Icons, The Royal Enfield Story* and *Janani: The Story of Yamuna*.

Hailing from Old Delhi, Raghav studied English literature at University of Delhi. His writings explore themes of loss of cultural identity, internal conflicts, post-colonial heritage in the 21st century, brown voices in a global community and man's reckless abuse of nature.

He is an ardent cricket fan and a travel and photography enthusiast. *Sita's Kitchen* is his first book.

Reach him at:
Instagram: @raghavkhanna24 and @sitaskitchenthebook
Email: raghavkhanna@outlook.com

Sita's Kitchen

Raghav Khanna

RUPA

Published by
Rupa Publications India Pvt. Ltd 2021
7/16, Ansari Road, Daryaganj
New Delhi 110002

Sales centres:
Allahabad Bengaluru Chennai
Hyderabad Jaipur Kathmandu
Kolkata Mumbai

ISBN: 978-93-5520-189-8

Third impression 2022

10 9 8 7 6 5 4 3

The moral right of the author has been asserted.

Printed in India

For Prem & Suraksha

Contents

1

The Midway Puzzle

Ben

The mountains at the farthest end wore a cap of snow, and the ones in the vicinity were draped in a cloak of pine. This was one of the most sublime landscapes I had ever witnessed. But none of that mattered. I was hungry and I was sleepy.

According to the map, the drive from Shimla to Kinnaur[1] was supposed to last six hours but five hours later we were barely at the halfway point. Cruising through the Himalayas in an SUV, I had taken the seat behind the chauffeur; a deafening honk and a sudden jerk tore through my slumber.

'Bhaiya![2] Who gave them a driving license?' I asked our driver after regaining my composure; a bus had brushed right past us. This was not a one-off instance; an array of manic vehicles had been driving past us with a presumption that

---

[1]Kinnaur: A town in the Himalayas
[2]Bhaiya: Brother or pal in Hindi

life was merely a video game.

'Don't worry, sahab![3] This is India; you'll get used to it,' he casually said, flipping the same manoeuvre on another passing vehicle. It was my first visit to India; I had barely got used to the fiery food and now I had to face this jigsaw driving style as well. A thirty-something man with a constant smile on his face, our driver kept himself entertained throughout the journey with a playlist of devotional songs and a steady supply of betel nut.

We had been on the move for two days. First, a non-stop flight from London to New Delhi, then hopscotching between overnight hotel stays, connecting flights and short drives—we finally were on our way to Kinnaur where my boss, Arun Mehra, was to inherit an apple orchard from his recently deceased grand-uncle.

Some people can be effortlessly suave with their fortunes. He wasn't inheriting a hardware shop or a potato farm; it was a goddamn apple orchard! How fancy would that sound on a Friday night fundraiser or during the Sunday brunch at the club?

But I confess, his charm influenced me to take up this job of being his executive assistant over the junior marketing associate role which the shipping company had offered. I did not have family savings to fall back on, forget savings, I barely had a family, and after five years of serving at an American fast food chain, I finally had two offers of what people considered proper jobs. The advertisements for both these jobs were placed adjacent to each other in the classifieds section of the newspaper, they were even offering the same pay and

---

[3]Sahab: Boss or master in Hindi

perks too but Arun's magnetism was perhaps the only thing the shipping company lacked. Then again, God really would have pulled a pun if I, Benjamin Atkinson of Greenwich, were to make sailors look great for a living.

Sitting on my left, with his noise-cancelling headphones on, Arun was relishing a bag of liquorice candies while being blissfully lost in views of the valley. We had been on the road for five hours straight but that did not perturb him at all; why would he care about such secretarial details anyway? He had hired me to do that on his behalf. Not just me, he had a squadron of people working for him at his London-based Italian restaurant, Bellissimo. In London, if you were a person of note then you would be a regular at his fine dining establishment. That made Arun, the forty-year-old restaurateur, a noteworthy man as well. Life for Arun was like a popular sport and he played it like a champion. But don't let his quintessentially Indian name deceive you—Arun was more English than most English. But telling that to my vocally conservative grandmother was a different matter altogether. When she found out that my employer was an Indian, she could not hide her displeasure. She belonged to a stealth cult where the English identity was still determined by colour and titles, not by birth and passport.

Born in London, into a family of Indian descent, Arun's forefathers were perfumers to the English royalty, and their perfumery at Oxford Street attracted the wealthiest travellers visiting London. Add to that, his time at Cambridge, his ancestry of colonial heritage, his discerning taste in scotch and ridiculously expensive teas, Sunday mornings at derby clubs and evenings on tennis lawns. This debonair life recently landed him a feature article in the UK edition of *The Esquire* and made him the darling of the neo-bourgeoisie of London, New Delhi and New York. Who wouldn't like a charming lad with a proper education, especially when he had given up his well-established family business only to start one of the most acclaimed and successful restaurants in the Kingdom? But to his credit, Arun was always the hardest worker on the floor and the sharpest brain in a meeting room.

But dear God, can you see your partisan ways? I could not even make up with Mark because my boss wanted me to accompany him to this obscure hill station.

People really undermine the power of peripheral vision. For the past half-an-hour, Arun had been vigorously texting, slipping in that wicked smirk every once in a while. After all, it was 10 a.m. in London and his twenty-four-year-old dusky jewel of a girlfriend, Zerena, would have risen from her white Egyptian cotton sheets and memory foam bed, the autumn dew frosting the panes of her Herne Hill apartment. And just as she would have thought of getting out of bed to brew coffee, a prolonged volley of messages from her lover would have confined her to the sheets.

How do I possess such vicarious details? Last month, Arun called me at midnight to find Zerena a new apartment. This was after an extremist religious group took offence to her walking the ramp for a lingerie brand. Not only did I successfully rescue Zerena through the fire exit while the violent protestors raged at the front door, I also found her the Herne Hill apartment, which was a significant upgrade from her suburban shanty. And then, I personally ordered the bed where my boss would plough her, went to shop with her for the decor and even called the internet agency on her behalf, all to prove how indispensable I am to Mr Mehra's *business*.

'Ben! You're such a darling!' She had said, thanking me with a peck on the cheek as soon as she was connected to the internet.

It was when she sunk her face into the glare of her smartphone, in the company of her '300k followers'—more than half of whom were bots chartered by the agency that represented her modelling interests—that I realized I would rather be Alfred to Arun than bestie with this bimbette.

'Bhaiya, stop here!' Arun sprung up abruptly, bringing the car to a sudden halt in the middle of the highway. Luckily there was no lorry behind us.

For the past two hours we had kept an eye out for an eatery for a quick snack. So far, the ones we had spotted seemed like a prelude to diarrhoea. Arun got out of the car and walked into a tiny café, perched along the road with a picture-perfect valley in the background.

'The Midway Café,' the tin board read. I followed him inside and surprisingly, the place was tastefully detailed. The walls were built of wooden planks, painted in a coarse shade of alabaster with scores of palm-sized colourful papers pasted on them. A shaft of late afternoon sun pierced through the window. The café had space only for four tables with four chairs each, they were covered with teal and fuchsia cushions and the shelves had an assortment of knick-knacks from all over the world. It seemed like a place for interior designers from Soho to be inspired by, only to then blend it with their high street sensibilities.

A frail man in his late fifties was busy dusting the counter. He seemed unperturbed by our presence. Arun had already found a seat by the giant window overlooking the valley where a stream was gently flowing through. I sat opposite my boss, staring at his striking jawline and the wall behind him, which was plastered with those colourful sticky notes. Upon closer inspection, I realised that these were testimonies from the customers. Between multiple thank-yous, merci-s and grazie-s, I even spotted some notes in Arabic and Russian; the place appeared to be popular with tourists, possibly backpackers like the ones we spotted along the highway, riding motorcycles or peeping out of bus windows.

Arun was leafing through the single page menu sandwiched between the wooden table and the glass top.

'Himalayan Aglio Olio,' he said condescendingly, without even bothering to look up. I too started reading the menu. I was astonished to find dishes of global fame, like lasagna and a set of sliders, all in this rural setting. It would have been one thing if this had been countryside Italy or even Britain, but roadside ravioli in this outback? It seemed a bit far-fetched.

While we were trying to solve this mismatching puzzle of a tiny European-esque café in rural India, the man on the counter approached us with two glasses of water, a pen and an order pad. His hands were rugged and his nails were stained at the root and black at the edges, a stark contrast to the immaculate and manicured hands Arun and I had. He placed the order pad in front of us and it read, 'Please write your order below in English.' Even the columns, for the customers to scribble down the item number and its name, were neatly aligned.

'Kaka[4], who owns this place?' Arun asked. The old man politely signalled that he was speech and sound impaired.

'Maybe the owner visits during lunch and dinner hours,'

---

[4]Kaka: A colloquial salutation for an elderly man

Arun told me confidently. 'They've even managed to get the spelling right,' he added with a sense of disbelief as he meticulously pored over the menu.

'Himalayan Aglio Olio and green tea for me,' he finally said and passed the notepad to me. It was blank. I was supposed to jot down both his order and my own.

'All right, boss,' I said softly and diligently set about writing his order, choosing the safer bet: a club sandwich and latté for myself. You can't get a sandwich wrong, can you?

It had been ten minutes since the old man had taken the notepad from us and disappeared through the door behind the counter. It was cold; we rubbed our hands for warmth and Arun was growing restless. He finally got up from his chair and started reading a Hindi newspaper.

'Can you read it?' I dared ask.

Arun was amicably quiet most of the time, but anything remotely insinuating his image as a modern renaissance man, or a conversation about food would get the better of his impulses.

'Of course, it's my native tongue. Dadima made sure I stayed connected to our roots,' he responded inattentively, without being offended by my question. Arun's grandmother had a profound influence on his upbringing. She had sent him to the elite Doon School in the Himalayan foothills to ensure that a part of his upbringing could be in India. Her brother, Arun's granduncle, had recently passed away, leaving his entire estate to Arun.

For over three years I have been working for this man, reporting on a daily basis—including some weekends and bank holidays—and yet the layers to his persona did not cease to intrigue me.

Another ten minutes had passed before the old man finally

returned with our order.

We were pleasantly surprised once again. The Aglio Olio was spiralled into a neat and petite pile on an ivory plate, the standard portion size of any professionally run restaurant. It was accompanied by a bottle of olive oil and some parmesan on the side. The club sandwich too was done just right with cold cuts, tomatoes and lettuce stuffed inside toasted bread and held together by cocktail sticks. Arun's reaction was priceless. He seemed almost disappointed. Perhaps, he had been ready to give me one of his usual sermons about how such fine food needed to be salvaged from bastardization. 'Other than the name, the dishes had no semblance to the original recipe,' he would have said. The man could go on and on about food; but who wouldn't if they made thousands of quids in this business on a daily basis?

We looked at each other for a moment before digging in. The very instant he took the first bite, Arun's expression changed and he was at a visible loss of words. He looked down again towards his plate and he said animatedly, 'Morels!' The man was a maniac for mushrooms. Hidden beneath his pile of Aglio Olio there was a petite arrangement of brownish morels with honeycomb heads. I knew the chef had him at morels.

'They're called Gucchi, sparsely found in this region, I can't believe it!' he said while making sounds of food-induced ecstasy.

'The garlic, it's seared and not burnt. Impressive,' he raved while he continued to relish the dish. 'Also, they didn't add oil to the pasta while boiling it, a mistake even some professionals make.'

Now it was my turn. Again, I chose my words carefully, already aware of how my boss felt about his meal.

'Quite amazing!' I said, 'The bread is perfectly toasted but the heat hasn't made the tomatoes soggy.' I was no epicure but I knew that the one thing that vexed Arun to no end was generalised comments about food, such as 'good' or 'bad'. He wanted you to dissect at as great a length as possible, the elements you liked and the ones which displeased. And over time, I had realised that his notion of complimenting a dish took on a pattern, something most chefs on reality television also employed.

At first, you state the obvious and expected, such as, 'The bread is perfectly toasted!' *Of course, the bread is toasted.* What else would you expect? For the yeast to smooch you? And then, after you have acknowledged that the cook is idiot proof, you say the most apparent thing which could have gone wrong but did not, such as 'the heat hasn't made the tomatoes soggy.' Even if they were soggy, *who cares?* For most people, a sandwich is well … just a sandwich. Couldn't we stop trying to find a Rembrandt in it for God's sake?

Arun was different; he had once expressed his passion for food while interviewing chefs, 'How could one not be passionate about something one does three to five times a day?'

To this day, I wonder if I should have spoken my mind that only a privileged few could afford to turn food into passion. Did we not still live in a world recovering from the pandemic? A world where over forty percent of deaths among children under the age of five were attributed to malnutrition? If I genuinely felt for the cause and was actively working towards it, maybe then I would have said something. As it was, Arun would have seen through the hypocrisy and figured out that this trivia was just a notification I had scrolled past.

By the time we were done with our meal, the old man

arrived with our tea and coffee. Just when the attendant was about to leave, Arun signalled for him to wait and scribbled something on a napkin in Hindi. I could not decipher what it was and neither could the old man—either the man could not read or Arun was bluffing about his fluency in Hindi.

Over an hour had passed since we arrived at this elfin café. By now, the winter sun had begun its premature and steadfast descent. There was a nip in the air and while we waited for the old man to return with our bill, I fetched my cardigan from the taxi. Bhaiya too was done with his tea and biscuits.

By the time I returned to the table, so did the old man. The details on the bill were handwritten in English and the puzzle of the Midway Café grew even more intriguing.

'Kaka, I want to meet the chef,' Arun said, conveniently forgetting that the man was deaf and mute.

The man made the same gesture and an incoherent sound.

Arun's frustration was obvious, he could not just leave without solving this mystery of finding near-gourmet food in the middle of nowhere. I took out my wallet to settle the bill but Arun placed a finger on the bottom of the receipt. 'Cashless payments only.' The hoary man at the café had surely embraced the ways of the new world. I instantly took out my phone and paid the bill with ease, showing him my screen as proof of payment. The man smiled gently before picking our empty cups.

By now, Arun was feeling fidgety and he headed towards the back door behind the counter.

With surprising vigour, the old man took two paces and barricaded Arun's advance. He was grunting in revolt; we had transgressed our limits and thankfully Arun understood as well. On another day, he would have been persistent.

The sun had set, but a dim violet hue still lingered in the sky as legions of fog descended down the hill and on to the highway. We reclined comfortably in our car and hit the road again. While I found a playlist to lull me, the Midway puzzle continued to perplex Arun.

2

Breakfast at Midway

Sita

'*Countryside mornings are devoid of any romance the tourists imagine them to have. The serene sunrises in reality reek of a chaotic urgency; the chirping of birds and humming of the village bard has long been replaced with pirated music of garish taste, playing loudly on speakers with extra bass, and the fabled earthy fragrance of the baked soil drenched by the rain is overwhelmed by labouriously distilled sweat, mixed with fumes of cattle dung.*'
I woke up with these thoughts clouding my brain like an internet browser with multiple open tabs.

'Indian School Certificate. Name: Sita Pandit, Father's Name: Hira Lal Pandit, English: 92, Mathematics: 84, Hindi: 81, Home Sciences: 82, Computer Science: 91.'

I glanced upon my class twelve marksheet hanging on the wall adjacent to my single bed. This marksheet, which back then used to be my biggest achievement, had started to seem less relevant with each passing year. Next to the marksheet was a photograph of my mother. I did not know when it was clicked, I was too small then, but the memories were forever etched in my heart—the happy ones and the ones of loss. My last recollection of my mother was a teary hazy glimpse of her motionless face buried beneath a pile of wood as a pyre consumed her; I was ten. Every time I thought of her, I had to move past that horrific sight to relive our time together. Memories, which were sealed by her kiss on my forehead every morning, coated with the ghee-laden rotis, which back then I resisted but now, I seek them in every meal; memories running with the melody of laughter from the evenings when we would skip the rope together or ride on the makeshift swing installed on the tree in our tiny lawn. I would often barge into the kitchen with a child's clingy curiosity and be with her while she cooked.

A gush of icy wind brought me back to the present.

Winter was setting in; the days were getting shorter and the nights terribly cold. My morning began with peeling potatoes for the breakfast menu. By the time the potatoes were put to boil, I was fully awake, but the sun was not out yet and it was time to graze the sheep, of which we had a dozen. The sheep of my district, Rampur Bushahr,[5] were among the most prized breeds of sheep in the region. Their wool made for fine blankets and their meat was tender as well. Brahmins[6], the community we belonged to, were largely vegetarians and meat-eating was a taboo—unless you were poor and living in the mountains where survival triumphed over scripture. As for me, I started relishing lamb around class nine and that

---

[5]Rampur Bushahr: A town midway between Shimla to Kinnaur in the state of Himachal Pradesh

[6]Brahmins: The upper caste Hindus

love had only grown since I had learnt to make meatballs and spaghetti. But for now, I had to stop dreaming about food and focus on the job at hand and watch the sheep clear their bowels. By now, Baba[7] too had gotten up to clean the café; he'd better have taken his medicines which I left on by his bedside, otherwise I would have to scold him again. He kept himself as his last priority.

The morning routine had been like this for the past five years, ever since I finished school and coaxed Baba into revamping his tea stall, 'Pandit-ji ki Tapri,' which served truck drivers on this route, into 'The Midway Café', which was aimed at the backpackers, trekkers and tourists who visited the valley. In a matter of weeks, enabled by multiple decor and upcycling videos, we transformed this place. Since then, life had been confined to the endless errands we ran within these hundred square yards of land facing the highway and hanging off the cliff. Baba still got to go out at night to have a beedi[8] or for the occasional glass of country liquor with his brother-in-law; he thought I did not know but I did, while I let him think that I did not. It was okay, they were not his dependencies and he deserved these little indulgences for all the hard work he did, not that we could afford anything else even if he wanted to. The society we lived in worked in your favour if you were a Brahmin but not if you were poor and it was even worse if you were a girl. So for me, the notion of stepping out did not exist beyond the morning graze with the sheep.

But it used to once, back when I went to school, taking

---

[7]Baba: Father in colloquial Hindi
[8]Beedi: A small local cigarette

the morning mile-long walk to the school with my friends, the sports classes, gossip during the recess and the same mile-long meander back with Lakshmi and Saroj; those were the daily joys I looked forward to. School was a lot of fun until that ominous day in class eleven when Lakshmi left school and never reached home. Her family lived at the foothills and we were all told that the wolves had taken her away; initially, there was a lot of media coverage around her disappearance but the journalists also stopped coming a month after her burnt body was found in the jungle. The incident was quickly erased from the memory of the media but it remained as a scar in the psyche of her family and friends. Since that day, the girls of the village stopped going out alone and just like the winter fog sets in, an eerie feeling had gripped everyone who knew Lakshmi.

I could still close my eyes and picture her standing in the school lawn, rim lit by the afternoon sun. I remember her every time a Hrithik Roshan movie came on television; she adored him and one of her biggest dreams in life was to meet him. Perhaps the most adventurous highlight of our school life was to bunk school and take the bus to the city to watch his film in a theatre. It was the first and the only time I had lied to Baba. I missed Lakshmi; her aspiration was to become a secretary in the city, like her elder sister. She probably would have become one by now had the wolves not taken her away.

By 7 a.m., Baba and I were done with half of our morning chores and we both sat at the café like customers and not the owners, making small talk through sign language or enjoying a moment of silence before receiving the relentless barrage of travellers. Baba would prepare ginger tea for the both of us while I made paranthas,[9] poha[10] or bread omelette for breakfast. I would do these preparations in bulk since these were the most sought-after breakfast items. Paranthas though were time agnostic, from 7 a.m. till 7 p.m., there was something about the buttery potato paranthas served with pickle and curd that put them on top of the list of the cravings the highway travellers had. I think they kept you full for long and were a safe bet on the road. As a cook though, I looked forward to the people who ordered from the Italian section on the menu so I could make those dishes, like the two travellers who had come yesterday.

I was anxious and excited; tourist season had finally begun after almost two years of deprivation. My supplies from the city were also replenished; I was to finally introduce three new breakfast items on the menu on a trial basis: Overnight Oats, Bircher Muesli, and Fruit & Granola Parfait with Yogurt. After breakfast, I wrote the week's special on the black slate while Baba did his routine of fumigating the café with sandalwood incense sticks. Then, I went downstairs to tend to the goat cheese I had set. I could hear noises from the shop; the first customers for the day had come.

---

[9]Paranthas: A type of Indian bread with assorted stuffings
[10]Poha: Popular Indian breakfast made with flattened rice

Ben

And there we were, back again; it had just been twelve hours since we had our supper here and my boss and I were back for breakfast. Well, breakfast was just a pretence, we both knew that Arun had to scratch his itch of finding out what about the café did not meet the eye. Last night we had truncated our drive and taken refuge at a roadside motel, a place which was well below Arun's and even my standards, but he wanted to stay close to the café. And today, Arun Mehra, who had rarely seen what 8 a.m. looks like, was waiting for me by the car at 7 a.m. Dressed in his chequered blazer with suede elbow patches, black polo t-shirt and khaki trousers, he was pacing around the parking lot. Have you ever had the privilege of acquainting yourself with a person who gets a t-shirt tailored rather than just buying it from a store? That was the kind of person Arun was. For him, everything had to be perfect or to his liking, and for him, the definition of perfect was everything that was to his liking.

'Accchoo!' I had just learnt the hard way that if you were staying below a certain grade of lodging, you should always check if the water heater is working before lathering yourself with soap. This was my tenth sneeze since morning and my germophobic boss had politely asked me to mask up in the car and sit at another table while we waited for our breakfast at the café. Sitting away from my boss was not something I did not want altogether; it meant I could enjoy my breakfast in peace and I chose a double egg white omelette and a latté on the side while Arun went beyond the table menu and ordered the 'Fruit & Granola Parfait with Yogurt' from the blackboard hung behind the counter.

The same routine—the old man serving us water, me writing both our orders and then the man disappearing for fifteen minutes—happened this time around as well and when our orders came, they lived up to the expectations set yesterday. My omelette was plain, devoid of anything worth mentioning in terms of presentation but the hot fluffy egg whites sandwiched between perfectly toasted bread felt like a warm embrace on this winter morning. Arun's parfait though was a sight to behold; served in a parfait glass, the dish looked like it was delicately assembled for a cover shoot with layers of hung yogurt, fresh berries, grapes and apples, all coated with multigrain granola and a hearty drizzle of honey. I looked at Arun, anticipating his reaction and I could not believe what I saw. This man, my boss, who was vehemently against the tribe of people who clicked a photo of their food before eating—'It takes the soul away,' he had once said—took a photo of the parfait before tasting it. After taking a bite, he got up from his chair and came and sat at the table where I was.

'It transports me to Paris,' he said, referring to the parfait. 'Come on try it,' he suggested. Just a while back he had been too apprehensive to sit next to me because I had the dreaded 'lurgy' and now he wanted me to take my spoon and dip it in his yogurt. I did entertain his whim and that one spoon drifted me into a quaint by-lane off Champs-Élysées, where you start a summer day with a parfait and a street performer plays an accordion in the background. It was a rather touristy description but that was exactly what the breakfast did to us, it made us tourists in one bite.

'Exceptional!' I agreed and looked at my boss, only to find him staring hard at the counter. By now a couple more customers had come to the café and the old man was busy serving them. The counter was left unattended and two lads, no more than twenty, rode in on a motorcycle and reached for the cashier's drawer. One of the boys took some cash from the drawer with a comfort that did not befit a thief. The old man returned to the counter and the boy who took the cash touched his feet, something I had seen a lot of Indians do; Arun too did that with his grandmother.

The boy who had taken the cash looked at me and snickered. '*Oye dekh, imported gur!*'[11] He said something to his friend in Hindi and from his tone, it sounded derogatory; Arun got up to confront him.

'Apologize,' Arun warned the two abrasive boys.

'Who the hell do you think you are?' they shot back, rolling up their sleeves in the anticipation of a fight. What happened next was straight out of a Bollywood film. Arun twisted the hand of the boy who had made the remark and pinned his head to the table, firmly keeping it there while holding him by his neck. He kept on twisting his arm and the young man started groaning in excruciating pain.

'Apologize, or I'll dislodge it,' Arun threatened.

'Sorry bhai ji, sorry bhai ji!'[12] the boy yelled and Arun set him free. By now, the shop owner had also arrived, concerned about what was happening.

'Mama ji[13] sorry!' The young man held his ears in front of the shop owner.

'Is he related to you?' Arun asked the old man, again

---

[11] A homophobic remark
[12] Bhai Ji: Brother, colloquially referred to a person of the same age but higher stature
[13] Mama Ji: Maternal uncle. Ji is a suffix added to show respect

forgetting that the man is speech and sound impaired.

'Yes, myself Bittu Sharma, I his nephew,' the young man introduced himself in halting English and with a sleazy smile. He extended his arm for a handshake while still aching from the twist.

'Never mind,' Arun muttered and asked Bittu to join us at the table. Bittu had a despicable vibe to his persona and it was not linked to the society he came from; one could instinctively say, he was not the best company to keep. He sat with us and offered a chair to his friend as well but one stern glance from Arun made sure the unnamed and equally sleazy lad kept himself apart.

'Who's the chef here?' Arun asked, unwilling to entertain any small talk with Bittu.

'My cousin sister, Sir. Why? Is anything wrong?' he asked.

'No. So where does your sister live?' Arun asked. Bittu looked a bit concerned and rightly so; Arun seemed desperate to meet the person behind all the fantastic food we had been eating; to an outsider, his intentions could seem questionable.

'They live here. We help in their bad times but now they doing very good,' Bittu said, trying to drive the conversation towards himself to gauge if there was any benefit for him to reap from the company of this affluent traveller.

'So tell me more about this café,' Arun asked, aware that asking to meet the chef would seem inappropriate. Bittu went on to make himself the protagonist of the story and told us about the café and its owners, but to his dismay, both Arun and I could deduce the relevant pieces of information. The old man who had been entertaining us was Hira Lal Pandit, or the locally known, Pandit Ji. He had been running a tea and snack stall for years but it looked nothing like this petite café and was more like every other shop we had crossed on the highway. A widower, Hira Lal focused on running this shop and raising his daughter with the best education he could afford. It required an occasional helping hand from his sister who was married to a local police constable and was the mother to this specimen, Bittu. Once Hira Lal's daughter finished her schooling, she started assisting him with the tea stall. Sita Pandit—we at last got to know her name—did not settle for the ordinary ways and appearances of her father's shop and revamped the place upside down. I was gobsmacked by this account. An Indian village girl was responsible for all the wonderful food we had been eating since yesterday! The 'how' of it still remained a mystery and Arun and I grew increasingly curious to meet this girl.

Sita

Baba was moving from one table to another, taking orders, bringing the customers their food and sometimes just checking on them to see if they were enjoying their breakfast; he was deliberately pretending to be busier than he actually was. It had become a routine; Baba would miss his morning medicine and I would come up to the café to check on him. I paced across the café and confronted him, face to face. At first, he looked away, making his guilt obvious and then, he looked at me with a child-like smile, a smile which never failed to evaporate my anger. I was his daughter, but at some point while he was busy parenting me, I started to become his parent as well. We filled a vacuum in each other's life; for me, he was my Ma[14] and Baba both, and from a very early age, I was tying the loose ends of his life like a mother or an elder sister would. I handed him his medicines; we were discreet in our confrontation to not create a scene in front of the customers.

While I was here, I thought I would see how the customers felt about the food. It was a busy morning. Tourist season had set in and all the four tables were occupied. There was a group of foreigners who wore their Ganesha t-shirts, shawls, beanie caps and khaadi[15] pyjamas, probably bought at a fortune from one of the bazaars in Shimla or Delhi; they had ordered sandwiches and tea for breakfast and were rolling tobacco at the table. They seemed sensible enough to not smoke inside the café where a big 'No Smoking' sign hung across the wall from where they sat. I do not know why people smoke, I tried it once after school and the bitter cough that followed permanently killed my temptation. On another table sat an Indian family—city folks, possibly from Chandigarh—the wife, husband and the elder son had their heads towed by their mobile screens while the younger son was playing with an electronic toy whose sound was puncturing the serenity of the morning. They were almost done with their paranthas and tea and I swiftly gave them the bill so the annoyance could end and the table could be free for the next customers. The third table was occupied by a man reading a newspaper. He had come in with his driver and they seemed to be in a hurry.

---

[14]Ma: Mother
[15]Khaadi: A fabric akin to linen

Perhaps he was a trader out on business and had little time for breakfast; during the off season, the apple traders from Shimla and Kinnaur kept our café afloat. But last year, even the domestic travellers could not help it; the first wave of the pandemic had not reached us but its economic devastation did—overnight, without warning—the influx of tourists stopped and along with them, stopped livelihoods for many like us. The economic famine ravaged through every knotted pouch women hid beneath their mattresses, every piggy bank children saved and every milligram of silver bought for such an event. We had to pivot back to serving truck drivers to have a steady source of income when the wandering curiosity of tourists had temporarily ceased. With the onset of winter, this road, which was not used to being idle, resumed to bear the weight of over-enthusiastic domestic tourists. Life was just returning to normal when the red summer came. We mountain folk are a hardy lot, but in a matter of a week, the second wave of the pandemic had people falling like someone had sprayed a pest killer within a colony of ants.

'Thank God the worst is behind us,' I reassured myself.

The business travellers were enjoying their ginger chai along with rusks and on the fourth table I saw my good-for-nothing cousin, Bittu, sitting with a vibrantly dressed foreigner and another man whose face I could not see but his hair was too neatly groomed to belong to this area.

'I hope he doesn't offend them,' I dreaded while approaching them to check if everything was all right and to separate my cousin from these customers.

'Arre didi[16],' said Bittu and I smiled, acknowledging him

---

[16]Didi: Sister

but avoiding to entertain a conversation in front of these strangers.

The foreigner was quite courteous. 'Hello, I'm Ben Atkinson. It's a pleasure to meet you,' he said, getting up from his chair and offering a handshake. I had my guard up, *'why is this tourist behaving so candidly?'*

'Didi, Ben ji is from London!' Bittu said with unwarranted enthusiasm. *'I have to stop him from talking further,'*

'Hi Ben, welcome to The Midway Café,' I interrupted, still wondering why a customer sitting with my cousin would spring up and introduce himself. The other customer at the table was Indian but his clothes and manners were that of a foreigner; he was suave, had sharp features and wore immaculately ironed clothes. I had not seen a man like him before. He was wearing an intense woody perfume; it was impossible to not notice it or not be charmed by that earthy yet elegant fragrance. He did not shy away from looking at me, observing me with a keen eye. I, like most women, was used to men staring at me but his gaze did not seem predatory and was rather curious in nature.

'Is she—?' Ben politely but cautiously tried to confirm my identity.

'Yes, she cooks all food. I also help her cook, but now I don't get time,' Bittu said. I wanted to correct him, all he ever did was eat the food I prepared for the customers and his cooking skills were limited to igniting the stove to light a cigarette, but I chose not to further highlight his incompetence. *'Don't argue with idiots, they drag you down to their level and then beat you with their experience,'* I had once read on the internet and the quote seemed apt today.

'Indeed,' I said with a faint sense of sarcasm, which went

above Bittu but landed well with Ben and the mysterious traveller.

'I'm Sita and I cook all the food here.'

'Your food is exceptional Sita,' Ben complimented.

'Thank you,' I said with a gentle smile.

'Can we have an Aalu Parantha, a Kulith ki Daal with Missi Roti, one Lamb Lasagna, one Minestrone Soup, one Chicken Foie-gras, one Kashmiri Gucchi Pulao, Bhey ki Sabzi[17] and a Tiramisu?' The suave man said with a calm but indifferent tone as he read out the menu. Though he was Indian, his accent was not from here. I did not know how to react. These guys had just finished their breakfast and were ordering food sufficient for eight.

'Sure ...' I said, when I was anything but sure of what was happening. 'Do you want it parcelled?' I asked.

'No,' the man replied, his tone was impassive but there was a polite and noble demeanour to him.

'Are you sure? We make everything fresh. This may take time,' I countered.

'It's alright, we have time,' he reinforced. I was perplexed, unsure of what this man was seeking, but looking at his appearance and mannerisms, it was not difficult to gauge that he could afford to entertain his whims and fancies.

And with that I went back to the kitchen, cooking this party-like order for this odd man while also catering to orders from the other customers. Thank god for Chotu, our neighbour's son who helped me in the kitchen for some pocket money. Even with the help, I knew I would have to be in the kitchen and cook all day. Not that I was complaining,

---

[17]Kulith ki Daal, Missi Roti, Bhey ki Sabzi: Indian food

how could I?' It was all I ever wanted—to be in the kitchen
and cook all day.

Ben

'Aren't toilets supposed to be relaxing? The Indian ones are
more intimidating than relaxing,' I freaked as I opened the
tin door of a tiny restroom adjacent to the café; it was built
of single file brick walls. The stench permanently burnt my
nostrils and I closed the door as swiftly as I had opened it,
forgetting the call of nature. My boss, on the other hand, was
unperturbed by anything except the food he was sampling. We
had already had the Aalu Paranthas, which were exceptionally
crisp and satiating. Then was the Kulith ki Daal, which was a
rather aromatic and complexly layered lentil soup. Arun told
me that Daal is actually a potage, commonly served as an
accompaniment to the main course across the country. The
remaining dishes which came were more to satiate Arun's
curiosity than our hunger.

Bittu had left after realizing that we were a couple of
foreigners exploring local food and had no gainful proposition
for him. Arun, on the other hand, did not stir from his chair,
he would think between each bite, deconstructing the food and
the flavour profiles in his head. In a manner uncharacteristic
of him, after a point he stopped discussing the food with
me and started scribbling notes into a leather diary he had
picked up from a fancy store at the airport. The lunch hour
had long passed and between breakfast and lunch all we did

was eat. Before Bittu told us about Sita, our premonition was that we would meet a couple where one partner would be Italian and the other, possibly Indian. They would tell us the story of how they met—the Italian partner would have been a chef travelling through India—and they had both decided to settle here in the lap of nature, away from the bustle of urban life, to cook for passion and a living. This certainly was far from the truth, as it is with most preconceived notions, and if we were to take a guess about who made all that food, an Indian country girl in her early twenties would be the last of our guesses. But there was something exceptional about Sita. She had large eyes and a sharp nose but her appearance was not what left a lasting impression. She was humble in her speech yet there was a deep-rooted and unassuming sense of confidence in her; and if one had eaten her food before meeting her, like we had, then one would only see her as a prodigy and an artist. Funnily and thankfully, the culinary world allowed twenty-somethings to be prodigies.

Personally, I was a tad bit envious of her sterling appearance. She had a pinkish fair complexion, which I noticed in a lot of people in this region. Her hair, though tied in a straight plait, had the shine and volume I could not achieve even after all the weekend conditioning and protein therapy. Although her curves were modestly defined, there was not an ounce of fat on her petite structure; all the rigour of the mountain life kept these folks in a shape that city folks splashed thousands of quids to achieve and I could not help but think: if I stayed here long enough, I could lose some of that underbelly.

Arun continued to eat. For a man who loved food but was also a fitness freak, this was an unusual day; he was behaving like a bottomless pit. When the Tiramisu arrived, I thought I could snag some to satiate my caffeine pangs but unfortunately there was just one serving of the luscious dessert and Arun did not even bother asking me if I would like to share it; he tried it once and then kept on digging into the glass cup like a man possessed.

'Rum! She has used Old Monk and not Marsala. Masterstroke!' He marvelled. How was I to react? I did not know how it tasted. By now, my bowels were giving up on me but the option of using the toilet was not really an option. Bhaiya had seen me close the toilet door in horror and he was observing me in my restless dilemma since then. He approached me with a plastic bottle filled with water and notoriously smiled.

'This is not a city, this is a village—nature is the toilet,' he said, sweeping his hand across the beautiful valley which we had been admiring as much as the food. The scissors of desperation cut through the garden of dignity; all along our journey I had been aghast to look upon people defecating in the open and now, I walked down the hill, among the shrubs and the weed, bottling up my pride and ready to unfasten my judgments.

Sita

'It's not foie-gras if it's not duck or goose. You may want to call it "Chicken Liver Pâté,"' the suave man said when I came up to the café. It was 3 p.m. and even the late-eating travellers were done with their lunch and there was a golden hour of lull before the rush of the tea-seekers would begin. Usually, Baba would go down to take some rest while I managed the counter with a flask of tea and coffee each for the one-off customers who would visit us during this hour. I put up a short and visibly fake smile in front of the man who now sat alone. His English friend, Ben, was missing from the scene. There was an awkward minute or so as we both sat alone at two different ends of the café; he was fidgeting with his pen and I sat with a stash of bills, scribbling inconspicuously in the ledger. We were conscious of each other's presence but found distractions to not become conscious of it. The needlessly honking trucks and one-off zipping cars echoed through the valley as they whizzed past on the highway.

'Did you like the food?' I asked.

The man fleetingly looked at me but did not react, though it did prompt him to ask a question in return.

'You made all of it?'

'Yes.'

'Without any help?'

'Yes'

'Yes to the help or to no help?'

'I mean yes, I have a boy who helps me do the mise en place,'

'Where did you learn that term?' he asked.

I too was curious to know why this man was *so* curious.

'From a book. I learnt it from Julia Child,' I replied, and the man who was so far aloof and selective in his conversation came and sat at my table.

'How do you know about Julia Child?' he asked, venturing further into a conversation.

'Well, I've read her books and seen most of her videos,' I said and my answers only heightened his curiosity. It was obvious that he did not expect me to fluently engage with him in a conversation, let alone talk about cooking techniques or some of the stalwarts of the culinary world.

'Who taught you to cook?' he asked and I could sense an undercurrent of disbelief in his questions. He was not convinced that *a village girl could cook* all this food.

'Was there a problem with the food?' I asked, refusing to respond to any and all the questions from this laat sahib[18].

'No, I didn't mean that.'

'Then, what did you mean?' I asked. Perhaps he was not used to being spoken back to and he took a moment to process my question; from here on, I had him off guard.

'The food … it was good,' he said. 'But not something one expects in the middle of the road in Himachal,' he added as an afterthought.

'So, if you ate this food in Chandigarh or Delhi, you would not be surprised?'

'No, it is not that.'

'Then what is it?'

'Perhaps it *is* that. It's unusual, unusually exquisite to be in the middle of a highway littered with traditional dhabas[19] to find a place where the decor, the menu and the food bring flavours from thousands of miles away,' he said.

His honesty was surprising; so far, I had thought of this man as someone who would be stubborn and unwilling to perceive something beyond his own judgement, but he

---

[18]Laat Sahib: A post-colonial slang for a self-assuming person
[19]Dhabas: Roadside restaurants

was proving to be otherwise. I accepted his statement as a compliment. His confession did set me to think about my own journey—the journey of a village girl who had never ventured beyond Shimla, who was not allowed to step out of the threshold after sunset, who, since the age of fifteen, was pressured by her relatives, neighbours and even strangers to get married, and probably would have been by now had my father not built that moat of safety around me. I did not have access to world foods nor could I afford to dine out, but to my misfortune, I grew up with an inextinguishable intrigue about food, the familiar and the unfamiliar kind, the dishes we eat locally and the cuisines foreigners ate as well. Had I been born a few decades ago, this curiosity would have become the tumour of regret in the depths of my soul, but it was the twenty-first century and lack of curiosity was the only thing which could have kept me from pursuing my interests. Thankfully, I had more curiosity in me than grains of rice in a plate of Biryani.

Ever since Ma left us, I acquainted myself with the kitchen, helping Baba with the chores and the odd washing, peeling and cutting. I only started cooking properly when I turned fifteen. The first few attempts were unbearable to taste. There was a prolonged period when everything I made, made for the dustbin and Baba never complained about the waste that accompanied such learning. Slowly, I started getting a grip on the recipes I was reading from the Italian cookbook I had, and with time, the food reached a point where I could taste it and say, 'Yes, I can serve this to the customers.' One afternoon, I painted a 'Foreign Food Available Here,' sign and hung it outside our tea stall. What was so far a trucker-only stop over became a pit stop for tourists. Even then, the only way for me to know if what I cooked was close to authentic or not was to ask the customers themselves, particularly the foreign travellers who came to the Himalayas for a trek or a retreat. Some would just scorn and stay aloof but most would give me a genuine feedback.

Emilia, a mountaineer from Italy was one such visitor.

'How was it?' I asked reservedly. I had just started serving basic pastas at the café. The pasta I served was of three kinds: spaghetti, fusilli and macaroni, since they were all available locally. I made them with red tomato and garlic sauce or the white sauce which had flour, cheese and milk. I was familiar with marinara, alfredo and bolognese, but for the customers and frankly for me, just a generic labelling of 'white' or 'red' did the task.

I would follow a recipe from the book or a video to a degree but invariably tweak it, giving it my own twist. The white sauce pasta came with a handful of green vegetables and the red had a pinch of the Indian garam masala. Now, when I think of it, it embarrasses me like a social media post from many years ago.

'You made it?' Emilia asked. Her face was red; the sun had baked her skin but she had a hardy frame like the Sherpas. From her backpack, shoes and the accompanying mountaineering apparatus, I could tell why she was here. I affirmed hesitantly.

'This is the food of my people,' she said in a thick accent. English was not her first language.

'Is it like original?' I asked, she smiled and nodded her head in a friendly manner.

'This much spice will kill an Italian,' she expressed. She was considerate to not insult my juvenile attempts.

'I cook back home and we welcome a lot of tourists at my restaurant in Rome. It's not fancy but it does the job,' she added.

'Will you teach me?' I asked without hesitation. She was only the second Italian cook I had met and I did not know when I would meet another. Bad weather had soiled her plans for mountaineering and over the next week, Emilia came to the café daily. She helped me with organizing our kitchen and the inventory and taught me the nuances of basic Italian fare.

'The best Italian food is made at its simplest. You have to resist the temptation to do more,' she told me while teaching me elementary techniques of how long I need to boil each kind of pasta, how to make the sauce with limited ingredients, even though it would feel incomplete because of the complexities Indians are used to.

'The first thing you need to do to make a more authentic version is to source olive oil. This oil is as far from Italian food as we are from Italy,' she said, looking at the bottle of vegetable oil I was using thus far. My time with Emilia laid the bedrock of my experimentation with Italian food.

'Come to Italy someday,' she said and embraced me tightly, and she then hugged Baba. He was at his most awkward. She sensed it and we both laughed.

I am still connected with her on Instagram and maybe I'll go and see her someday. She also introduced me to the wider world of Pinterest and Instagram, which opened new windows for my cooking and provided me with great inspiration to revamp our tea stall into a café. We did not have any funds so the change was gradual. It involved a lot of upcycling—the wooden planks on the walls were taken from an old house demolished for reconstruction, we painted them ourselves so it lent a coarseness to the walls, which then became their character. The cushions were stuffed with cotton from second-hand mattresses and the covers were stitched from old bedsheets dyed at a nearby dyer. The table and chairs too were made by the carpenter from our school; thankfully, we had access to good timber.

And while my cooking and the café had started taking form, six years ago, something monumental happened in my life. I got high-speed and unlimited internet at an affordable price. And that was not all—e-commerce websites started delivering at our doorstep; everything I wanted to learn or yearned to own was just a click away. For a girl who had never travelled, that was her login and password to follow her pursuit. I would spend all my bandwidth just learning about food, intrigued particularly by the Italian cuisines and the cooking techniques—from street food to fine dining experiences, voraciously watching videos made by chefs, both professional and amateurs, switching on subtitles when needed. I was astonished that all this knowledge was available for free.

Thankfully, by then our café was also doing well and every fortnight I would save a sum of one thousand rupees to allow myself an indulgence: a utensil, a knife, a mixer, a strainer, a measuring cup or an assortment of items my heart desired. Sometimes I went beyond my allowance, but it was not before I realised that these were not indulgences but investments, and the repertoire of my cooking and my menu increased with each purchase. Of late, I could even order some ingredients online, but most of the inventory I needed to cook with, was available fresh, and for things like pastry sheets and pastas, I was fortunate that our neighbour and Chotu's father, Surinder

Chacha[20] worked in the city. I would write to him with my requests, and of course, pay him later.

'Tell me one thing, how did you develop an interest in food?' the man asked. I had just re-lived my life of the past six or seven years and was unwilling to narrate it again, so I chose to tell him the point much before all of this, when I, a little girl of ten, was transformed by a man and his book.

'It was about twelve years ago, there was no internet and no smartphones. I clearly remember that afternoon. It was scorching hot and there was no electricity; back then, power cuts were a daily affair. Baba was at the stall and I had just come back from school. In those days we did not serve food, but only had tea and snacks on the counter. There was this foreign couple who had stopped by for tea. They were driving a Gypsy and when they came to the counter, the woman said she was extremely hungry; her belly jutted out like it contained a melon. Baba could not understand them, so with the help of broken sign language and using me as a makeshift translator, her partner conveyed their limitations and urgency to us. They seemed warm and desperately in need of some food. The man realised that we did not have much to offer but we had what he needed—a stove and a vessel. So, he requested we bring him some garlic, chillies and oil, which we had. From his satchel, he took out some spaghetti he had been carrying along. And there I stood at the counter, mesmerised by this tall white man, rolling up his sleeves and cooking for his love; from that day, I didn't want to believe in the story of a knight in shining armour but that of a chef in an apron. The couple were rather affectionate

---

[20]Chacha: Paternal uncle or an man close to one's father in age

and they saw me lingering around them. Though the pasta was barely sufficient for one, the pregnant woman invited me to share it with her.'

I recalled all this as my eyes welled up, remembering the incident minute by minute as it had unfolded all those years ago.

'At some point during the meal I stopped eating and went around with my games, only this time I was not playing with dolls but lit up a stove, trying to imitate the man. When Baba discovered me, he pulled me away and gave me a tight slap. Touching the stove was forbidden. I don't blame him, I could have burnt the whole place down. But thankfully, the foreign couple came to my rescue. I was too young and I do not know what the woman told Baba using signs and some instincts but what I clearly remember is the man squatting down, wiping the tears off my cheek and telling me, "*If you want to cook, you must learn how to do it,*" and then he reached for his satchel, took out a cookbook and handed it to me. *The Silver Spoon* was a pictorial Italian cookbook written in English and I was at a stage where I was just learning how to read. The curiosity ignited by those pictures of gnocchi, spaghetti, tortellini and all those types of cheese made sure that I paid full attention to my English classes so I could read this book.'

Waving away the memories, I saw the man standing silently, looking at me, trying to gauge if I was really speaking the truth or taking him for a ride.

'Can you cook something in front of me?' he had the audacity to ask when all that I had done since the morning was only to cook for him.

'Don't you think it's rather strange that you have been

eating here since yesterday, ordering unusual pairings from the menu, asking about my life history while not even telling me your name?' I asked in return.

'Arun Mehra,' he said, introducing himself with the casual flare of a film star.

'Alright Mr Mehra, so far I was happy to cook for you and to tell you about my life as well. I love talking to our guests, it's a good break for me, but that's going to be it. I don't intend to let a stranger into my kitchen,' I said firmly, unwilling to entertain his request.

'Pardon our transgressions but I believe this calls for a proper introduction,' Ben suddenly arrived with an inexplicable relief on his face.

'Arun and I are from England. We are here on some business and when we saw your café, we wanted to explore it. When we ate the food you made, it was compelling enough for us to postpone our other engagements and try more of what you make. Mr Mehra owns Bellissimo in central London, the most famous Italian restaurant on the island. So yes, while unusual, his request to see you cook is purely professional in nature,' Ben explained, while looking at Arun to support his argument.

'Yes, he's right, I am simply intrigued by what you make and how you make it,' affirmed Arun.

It was funny how his request seemed more like an instruction. Now that I had gotten to know his true identity, my heart was racing with excitement. *A man who runs a restaurant in London likes my food and wants to see me cook!* Why he wanted to do that perhaps he knew best, but why I wanted him to do that was simply to seek professional validation. I had had hundreds of customers loving my food and complimenting me and at first, it was exciting but after a point it became the norm. But for an international restaurant owner to do so, meant the world to me. It meant that every night when I would dream, I could tell myself that those dreams were not delusional.

'Let me ask Baba,' I said.

That evening, for the first time since Emilia, I allowed a stranger to enter my kitchen. The space was congested and Ben was peeping through the large window overlooking our small kitchen garden where I grew herbs. Baba was seated in that garden and Arun stood beside me in the narrow confines of my kitchen, keenly observing what I was doing. He asked me to make the same Aglio Olio he had last night. I did so and he tasted some of it and then kept it aside. Then he asked me to make a lasagna and the same course followed. He tasted the second dish and then the third and after the third, he thankfully stopped. The sun had set and the rattling of insects grew louder.

'It's hot here. I'm getting some air,' he said and stepped out. He casually lit a cigarette, without the need to seek our permission. He noted the desire to smoke in Baba's eyes and he offered him a cigarette as well. In the dim light of the departed sun, against the backdrop of the busy highway, he stood carefree, now looking much more at ease than he had been throughout the day. Even though he was smoking, he kept his distance from me and Ben, the non-smokers, consciously exhaling the smoke sideways so we would not be overwhelmed by it.

'Work for me,' he said, casually exhaling and then taking another drag from his rapidly depleting cigarette. I was not sure whether he was making an offer, asking me a question or giving me an order like I already worked for him.

'What?'

'Work for me, in London.'

'No!' I reacted instinctively. I had not even processed what he was proposing.

'Why not? You have talent—a gift I'll say—and with some training, you can explore your true potential.'

'No,' I declined again.

'But you said you loved cooking and I am taking you to the world's best city to do it.'

'Best for whom? This is my home and this is where I will cook!' I replied.

'Think about it. Ben will be here tomorrow to help you with the details of the offer,' he said.

'I have thought about it and I am declining your offer,' I asserted, putting an end to this conversation. Arun did not respond. He stubbed his cigarette in the ground, stomped it with his foot and walked towards the iron stairway. And just when I thought it could not get any worse, Baba, who was done with his cigarette, approached Arun and asked for a couple more. At first, I thought I would intervene, but I refrained, not willing to give the man another opportunity to strike up a conversation or to persuade me to accept his proposal.

After both of them left, Baba was busy winding up the café for the day. Normally, I would assist him but tonight I just could not, the cramps were unbearable. As I lay in bed, I felt my legs dissolve into the mattress. My heels were aching from all the standing, but that was not what was bothering me. Dreams can be intimidating. I could not help but imagine the streets of London, walking through them every morning as I went to work, just like in a scene from an English film. The audacity of my dreams grew, I was wearing a chef's coat and cooking for the connoisseurs of fine food. But was I really worthy of that life? Or was this man driven by a fleeting whim which would evaporate the moment he was back in the city? And even if all this was to happen, what about Baba?

3

No Means No

Ben

O ne of the most identifiable markers of country life is the crowing of a rooster at the crack of dawn, something the likes of city rats like me had only seen as children in our illustrated books or caricatured cartoons. Today, after twenty-six years of being familiar with the world, I finally experienced it for myself. I was ready with my bags when Arun casually asked, 'What are the bags for?'

'Aren't we checking out?' I asked, fully aware that we were doomed to stay here. The real question was, for how long?

'No, we are not! Leave your bags at the counter,' he said and hurriedly sat in the car. Thanks to Bhaiya who rushed to my rescue, collected my bags and kept them in the boot. What were we getting late for anyway? It seemed like Arun had forgotten why we had come to India in the first place and what he did back in London.

'Call my uncle's lawyer and tell him we're unable to make it today as well,' he ordered, referring to the orchard he was to inherit. I nodded in agreement. Frankly, what more could I do with this whimsical child of a boss?

'Also call Gabby, tell her to hold the fort a bit longer,' he said and then he slid down the car window to light his morning cigarette. Once a chain smoker, Arun was now restricted to three cigarettes a day: one before he started work, one after lunch and the last with his high tea. This, of course, excluded the time when he was travelling or on his social outings, of which he had plenty and where he would light a cigarette or a cigar depending on the company he was with. It did not take much to predict where we were headed. Fifteen minutes after we left the hotel, we reached The Midway Café again.

We sat at one of the tables. Hira Lal was not to be seen around and after a couple of minutes, the father and daughter emerged from the door behind the counter.

'You're back?' Sita said loudly, unamused to see us.

'Is this how you welcome your guests?' Arun asked with a rare smile, a change from his usual dogmatic tone.

'No means no, don't you get it?' said Sita. I had never seen someone talk so assertively to Arun. Beneath her unassuming five-feet-something appearance there was a girl of grit; we had already learnt of her culinary skills, but what struck me as truly remarkable was how self-aware she was, something most people failed to achieve throughout their lives.

'We are only here to have breakfast,' said Arun and without arguing any further, Sita went about with her chores. She was wearing a mahogany salwaar-kameez[21], something Arun's mother Lata also wore quite often.

---

[21]Salwaar-kameez: Indian ladies attire, not a saree but a long shirt with pyjamas

'Good morning, Ben, what would you like to have?' she came and asked, handing me the order pad. I could smell that basic, general store greenish soap on her, the one our hotel also had. She had just taken a bath but did not wet her hair. She treated us just like any other customer, courteous when she approached us for the order but making us feel invisible in the interim until our food arrived. I ordered some scrambled eggs with my usual dose of latté while Arun ordered chai and Poha. We ate our breakfast and it was amusing how quickly surprises become expectations. We expected these ordinary dishes to taste extraordinary after what we had been experiencing for the past two days. The meal was over quickly and we had no other reason to linger on but when the bill came, Arun tried to act cheeky.

'Do you have a feedback section?' he asked Sita.

'We do,' she handed him a colourful postie, similar to the ones plastered on one of the walls.

'The food is global, so too can be the chef,' Arun wrote on the paper. He raced us from the table to the car in such an effortless way that neither did we seem anxious to be waiting for her to see the testimony, nor did we miss out on her reaction by leaving prematurely. When we were at the threshold of the café, Sita peeped at the note, stopped her smile before it slipped past her lips and looked back at Arun, who was only looking at her.

Post-breakfast we drove aimlessly and come lunch, we returned to the café. Sita was nowhere to be seen and presumably so, the café was teeming with hungry travellers and we had to wait for a bit before a table was vacant.

The concept of good food is a relative one. You have to pace it out sufficiently with mediocre meals to truly relish the outstanding ones. By now we had an overload of too-good food for us to feel equally excited upon reading the menu. Arun ordered a plate of goat cheese and arugula salad, back to his way of balancing indulgences with mindful eating and though I was preparing myself to order spaghetti and meatballs, I too felt I could do with a light lunch and opted for the same salad.

The place found a lot of favour from its customers. Most would order more than they could eat, I guess it was because of the taste—it was not one of those places with a star rating, nor was it a legendary outlet or some place that many tourist portals wrote about, but it was one of those places where if you had eaten once, the taste or at least the memory of that taste would linger on for years to come. Arun's anticipation could be felt at the table. His eyes constantly returning to the door behind the counter and the fidgeting of the pen only grew faster as our lunch came to an end. Before leaving, he left a sealed note for Sita; I could not gauge its contents but it was a short one.

Come evening, we were back for supper and between lunch and supper we did what we had done between breakfast and lunch: nothing. Hira Lal too was growing suspicious of our intentions and greeted us indifferently by leaving the order pad on the table. What we ordered was no longer important but the meal wound up faster than we had hoped and Arun's desperation was getting the better of his judgement; he could be termed a borderline stalker by now. Arun took care of the bill and left a hefty tip. One thing I noticed about the place was that while the food was at par with some of the fine restaurants we had eaten at, it was awfully inexpensive. We could finish a meal for two for less than five quid; elsewhere that would be half the tip! As we got out of the café, Arun lit a cigarette and stood on the small patch of gravelled land separating the highway from the café. Hira Lal had finished resetting the furniture and was looking at Arun who was almost done with his cigarette. From afar, Arun took out his pack and offered Hira a cigarette which he accepted instantly. The two stood outside the café, enjoying their cigarettes. Soon, Arun was on his third while Hira lit his second.

The evening was unusually quiet despite us being in front of a highway, as if all the people and the sun were done with their day and had slid into a warm quilt with a hot cup of soup. I certainly was looking forward to that as a respite from this bone-freezing dusk, waiting for my boss to run out of patience or cigarettes. The door behind the counter opened with a thunderous thrust and Sita stormed out.

'You city folks can stoop to any level!' she blared. Hira Lal dropped his cigarette and was petrified to see his daughter. She took her father by the hand and pulled him back like he was a mischievous kid.

'It's not that—' Arun tried to respond but she interrupted.

'Shut up and don't come back here!' she fumed, storming away the way she had come.

Ben

It had been two days since the confrontation when that twenty-something village girl told one of the top restaurateurs in the UK to shut up. We did not go back to the café but we did not go anywhere else either. She was either angry to see

Arun encouraging her father's smoking or she took offence to the note he had written.

'I don't know when he's coming back. You're the boss, Gabby, do what needs to be done,' I said over the phone, trying to avoid palpitations from all the work piling up because Arun was supposed to be back in London by now. He had been locked in his room for two days, selectively responding to texts if they were business-critical.

'We've lost our star, Arun!' I bore the bad news from the other side of the door. There was no response and then he opened the door, dressed in his jacket, polo t-shirt and trousers. He started walking through the corridor, leaving behind a trail of his oak and amber cologne.

'I don't need the validation of a goddamn tyre company to tell me how good my food is!' he yelled as he stepped down the hotel stairs and headed for the car. It was half-past-three in the afternoon and we were headed for the café again when we spotted Bittu on the road. He was riding his motorcycle with a saffron bandana across his forehead and a flag hazardously tied to the back of the motorcycle. He was following a procession of other bikers with similar flags; they all were yelling some kind of slogan at a pitch which would rupture their chords.

'Stop!' Arun said, rolling down the window.

'Bittu Bhai, how are you doing? Would you care to show us your village?' asked Arun.

The imbecile was surely not used to this sort of attention from a man of Arun's stature, for he obliged instantly. We trailed after his bike for a few hundred meters before he joined us in the car.

'Sir, how do you like our Rampur Bushahr?' Bittu asked.

We had been driving with him for a while and he had shown us some temples, the Padam Palace, the suicide point, the lover's point and his college, among other places in this district.

'It's beautiful. I have never seen such a beautiful town,' said Arun with such subtlety that it was beyond Bittu to gauge the sarcasm; he took his words at face value.

'That it is, Sir. But you must also go to Spiti and Manali[22], you get good stuff there, something you foreign people also love,' he said, sleazily elbowing me in the ribs. I did not grace his insinuation with a response.

'They are good ... but this place ... this view is one of the best,' Arun replied.

'That it is, Sir, everything about Rampur Bushahr is best, Sir.'

'Indeed. The view, the air, the greenery and even the food,' said Arun. Bittu concurred again.

Very rarely do I get miffed with someone, but Bittu made it to that list with his effortlessly annoying manners. He was more judgemental about my appearance than my furiously fundamentalist grandma was when I came out.

'Yes, Sir. The food is good, Sir. But did you tried McDonald's? It's fifteen kilometres away.'

'But the food at your Midway Café is pretty good too.'

'Yes, Sir. Sita Didi is best cook, Sir.'

'I wonder why she doesn't work at a good restaurant in the city?'

'Sir, she get many offers from Shimla and Chandigarh. But she loves Hira Mamu very much, she will not leave him and go away,' he explained and Arun and I looked at each

---

[22]Spiti and Manali: Tourist destinations in Himachal Pradesh

other like medieval sailors would look at each other upon sighting land.

'Didi was topper in school. Got admission in Delhi to study cooking but last minute she decided not to go and be with Mamu,' he added.

Her blatant reservations overriding that immense love for food now made sense, it was not the idea of taking up a job at Bellissimo which she was averse to, but leaving her father.

'Do you know sign language?' Arun asked suddenly.

'No Sir.'

'I do, Sir!' revealed Bhaiya, who had been a fly on the wall so far.

'What?' we both said, collectively shocked.

'Yes, Sir. My son cannot speak, so me and my missus learnt it,' he said.

Arun immediately asked him to drive to the café. We were losing light. It was 7 p.m. and The Midway Café would shut soon. Not only would Bhaiya become our key to the conversation, he had also outdone our expectations. Before going to the café, he dropped Bittu back to his motorcycle. Frankly, it was good riddance and I think Bhaiya felt the same. We rushed to the café as fast as we could but the lights were already out.

'Damn it!' cried Arun.

And then, we saw a shadow move behind the dark counter—a moving car threw light on the man's face—it was Hira, his eyes and every wrinkle defined by the passing light beam.

'Ask him if we can get some tea,' Arun nudged Bhaiya who got out of the car and conversed with Hira in sign language. The headlights of our car were lighting the café. Hira had just folded operations for the day. After initial reluctance, he agreed and put the kettle on the stove. Arun too got out of the car, instinctively pulling a cigarette out, but just before lighting it, kept it back in the pack. Left alone in the car, I felt unnerved by the eerie solitude and joined the others.

'Tell him I want to talk,' Arun asked Bhaiya to translate, which he did. We all took our cups of tea and pulled some stools from the café and sat outside, slightly angular from the car's front so the headlamps did not blind us.

'The tea is good,' said Arun and Bhaiya translated. He was restless, fighting the pangs to not have a smoke accompany his cup of hot tea on this chilly evening.

'Your daughter, Sita, is gifted—she has flavours on her fingertips,' Arun pressed, and the old man blushed with pride.

'This is my restaurant in London,' he said, taking out his mobile and showing him some photographs of the restaurant and himself.

'My family too is from India, in Delhi. We still have a house in the old city but nobody lives there anymore,' he said and Bhaiya kept translating. So far, Hira had not asked a question and we were blindly relying on Bhaiya to convey what we said.

'I see chefs every day. A dozen work for me and many-a-dozen want to,' Arun said with a dramatic overture, taking a sip of his tea. 'But food is not like making a product in a factory; it is an art, the most essential art in our lives,' at this point I nudged Arun to not give a sermon but strike a bargain. He could unintentionally, but out of habit, become philosophical while talking about food. Thankfully he got the point.

'This opportunity will change your and your daughter's

life, but most importantly, it will give her talent the platform it deserves. Do you not want to see your daughter in a place where she is happy and safe, even after you?' he prompted, and right on cue, Sita appeared through the backdoor.

'Don't you get it? No means No! Stop troubling us!' she was exasperated, irritated and even helpless to see us here again.

Arun got up, held her hands and looked straight into her eyes. 'Your Baba. He can come with us to London.'

It was as if someone had possessed him and immediately after speaking, he let her go and seemed slightly embarrassed to have held her hands in the first place.

Father and daughter looked at each other, furiously conversed in signs before she held his hand and went downstairs.

Sita

'*I don't believe his audacity!*' I thought as I took Baba down the stairs.

We sat in his room. He was sheepish, not willing to discuss anything and was expecting me to start yelling at him.

I conveyed that we should stop entertaining that man.

'Why?' he signed and frankly, I did not have an answer. Barring that cigarette incident, Arun had only been respectful with his offer; persuasive, yes, but not aggressive. There is a fine line.

'I should have listened to your aunt and got you married,' Baba signed jokingly. He was not wrong. He stood against the tide of society to give me the space to be who I wanted to be. Today, I was in a place to reject an offer to cook in London, but a few years ago, the best I could have done was find a boy whose village was close to Shimla. Those boys were a keeper among the girls from my school, that was the furthest our aspirations could travel.

'*Do I want this?*' I asked myself, possibly for the hundredth time over the past few days and while all of me was screaming to do nothing else but take up this offer and cook, the same part of me ran an album of thumbnails in my head—of my life with Baba; the horror of imagining Baba here without me would rip through my heart.

'*How can Baba travel with us? And if he can, then can I do this?*' I was lost in my own thoughts when Baba held me by my shoulders.

'From the day your mother left us, I only had one dream,' he signed and his eyes welled up. 'That you could follow yours.'

We both hugged each other and wept. Was this weeping out of joy or sadness, I could not comprehend, but it certainly was out of all the love and gratitude I had for my Baba.

'How do we do this?' I sent Arun a text.

Three days ago, he had left his number for me with a note, which read: 'The world is waiting to eat this food. If you ever change your mind, call.'

Ben

It was still dark outside but intuitively I knew that the night was over. The barrage of knocks on my door would not stop. I got up and had a nerve freeze upon stepping out of the quilt, barefoot on the uncarpeted floor.

'Get ready, we need to go,' Arun barged in and spoke. At this point I did not want to show any intrigue, how would that matter? I would have to go anyway.

'Give me ten, please,' I said, hoping Arun would leave as swiftly as he came so I could brush, wash my face and change.

'Hurry up. See you downstairs,' he said and left. I got ready as fast as I could and from the window of my room, I could see Arun pacing up and down in the lawn where our car was parked. Within five minutes we were on the road and by the time the first rays of light were cracking the sky open, we had come to The Midway Café; it was still shut. The fog on the road had an eerie but romantic charm to it—you would want to be here, taking a walk with your lover—but every time a pair of headlamps tore through that blanket of fog, it reminded you why that walk would not end well. I saw Arun standing in the corner adjacent to the counter; he was texting. It was not to his lover, Zerena, he was too tense to be in pleasure. About ten minutes later, Sita and Hira arrived and soon we all were sitting in the café with our cups of tea.

'So, you agree?' Arun asked and Sita nodded with uncertainty. I do not know what had happened last night after we left but thankfully, we would not have to stay here any longer.

'Ben, I'm leaving you in charge of getting their paperwork done. Bring them to England,' Arun said, throwing a bucket of ice-cold water on my hopes of seeing Mark anytime soon.

'I have some questions,' Sita said. 'Where would we stay?'

'An apartment of course, Ben will find you a good house close to the restaurant,' Arun said.

'I have never cooked in a restaurant other than mine.'

'I'm aware,' said Arun.

She asked a couple more questions around the logistics of it all, which Arun directed towards me, and once all their immediate queries were answered, Arun got up, shook hands with Hira Lal who took Arun's outstretched hand in both of his hands and shook them vigorously. He then turned to Sita and said, 'The kitchen at Bellissimo welcomes you.'

We paid our bill for last night and today and left the café. In the car, Arun instructed me to get her employment contract, terms of engagement, remuneration, visa and other paperwork in place, plus he told me to stay here till they were able to relocate. I am certain it was not a part of the company's relocation benefits, but he left me here to ensure that she would not change her mind.

Sita

I loved the Mall Road in Shimla. Lately, I had been too busy to come here but the uphill walk among the shops and eateries had always been an experience to cherish. Ben and I were out shopping. It had been four weeks since I had accepted the offer and Ben had helped us with all the paperwork. Neither Baba nor I had a passport or tax papers. For us, travelling abroad did not even exist as a concept to ever think about it. Thankfully, the application process was digitized; we had to visit Shimla a couple of times to update our records—that was all done now. The next challenge was to get our visa, for which we travelled to Delhi. Our appointment had taken place two weeks ago and I thought we should take the time to do some shopping.

'How cold is it in London?' I asked.

'As cold as here, but we have heating systems,' Ben said, rubbing his hands together vigorously. We were a week or two away from snow and I bought him a pair of gloves and a traditional Himachali cap. We shopped and ate together; he deserved this time out after all the legwork he had done on our behalf. I bought some new clothes for myself and a wool blazer for Baba as well.

We then went to the local wax museum. I wanted to click a selfie in front of Hrithik Roshan's statue and insisted that Ben join as well.

'Gosh! my blackheads!' he said, looking at the photograph.

'By the way, who is he?' he asked. I was surprised he did not know who Hrithik Roshan was.

'He is India's most handsome actor!'

'Eye candy, for sure,' he said. We then went to The Embassy Bakery for some cakes and coffee. Back when I was in school, I could not afford to eat at this place but their apple strudel appeared to be truly a work of art and I loved their wooden decor.

'This looks like a quaint English town,' he said, looking at the church and the cobblestone pathways.

'Shimla was India's summer capital during the British Raj,' I said. He seemed surprisingly naive about the British occupation of India. I was steadily gaining new insights into world history. Having started with textbooks and culinary books, books at large had become my window to the world. Even though I was yet to travel, most of the places I had read about or seen on the internet seemed more familiar than it would to a tourist and I felt just a notch short of being their citizen. On any random afternoon, I would do an internet search for the most beautiful village in Switzerland, the biggest city in America or the eastern-most part of Japan. England and London, in particular, were always on my search history. The elders in our village had a strange fixation with the British land, and for the ones who were as old as the pine trees, who had seen the times of the Raj, they spoke of the Britishers as if gods had walked amongst us.

Ben was looking at me; I was lost in my thoughts. I had forgotten what we were talking about. 'Let's go?' I asked and he nodded.

It was late afternoon. We were on our way home, before it got dark. I was in the car with Ben and Jitender-ji, the driver who Ben referred to as Bhaiya. I got a text.

'This is to inform you that your passport and visa are ready for collection.'

I was finally going to London!

4

Hello London

Sita

'Protect us Shiva, Protect us! Protect us Shiva, Protect us!' I was whispering with a petrified stammer as the double-decker plane raced along the runway. The wheels left the ground, now it was upon the wings to take us onward and upward. For someone who had only travelled in trains and buses, this experience was one of many firsts. We were seated in the business class.

'Can I see the bill?' I asked.

'It's on the company,' Ben said from across the aisle.

'I want to see!' I insisted; he was reluctant but finally, he gave in. I had to read the figure thrice to check if I was reading an extra digit, we did not make that kind of money in a year! Baba was frightened to be locked in a steel capsule, but the fascination of being airborne was getting the better of his fears. He urged me to take the window seat and though he did not know how to read English, it did not stop him from browsing through a couple of magazines he had picked up from the boarding section. The face shields were an annoyance, but then, we undermine our ability to become habituated with things which were once alien.

The flight attendant offered us warm towels, Baba took one and cleaned the headboard, the armrests and other nooks within our seating space. I waited to see what the other passengers would do; some cleaned their hands and arms with it, while some just left it on their face like a mop on the floor. I did the latter and all the tiredness trapped in my face released in an instant; looking at me Baba too tried to do the same but I stopped him—his towel had scrubbed on all the visible parts in our cabin!

Ben had his rainbow-coloured sleeping mask on; we were flying above a blanket of clouds and the cabin crew started taking requests for the meal. The menu was available on our mobile through a QR scan and had three cuisines to choose from. There was Indian, with a photograph of Sanjay Seth on the menu, India's favourite chef on television. Then there was Graham Reed, the most intimidating chef I had seen on the internet, and the last was Marco Russo. He was not on television much but I had read about his preservation movement for authentic Italian food.

For Baba, I chose Dahi Kebabs and Palak Paneer[23] from the Indian section. I was unsure if he would be willing to try any other cuisine. Even back at home, he had what I made but his satiation only came from the food he was familiar with. For myself, I chose from Russo's offerings: a Barley Soup, which came with an assortment of breads, followed by a Pan-Seared Norwegian Salmon; it was my first time eating a salmon. In

---

[23]Dahi Kababs and Palak Paneer: Indian dishes

Himachal it was unavailable where we lived and the five-star hotels of Shimla were a luxury I could not afford. The food tasted good but was a notch below my expectations. What stood out was the presentation. Two fillets of salmon were placed in a cross section, one on top of another, with a light drizzle of lemon butter sauce and it was garnished with micro greens.

'*Less is more and make a habit of layering,*' I recalled from one of the food plating tutorials I watched on YouTube.

For the dessert, I chose Pandoro, a star shaped cake with a generous dusting of sugar, which was accompanied with an Almond Gelato. It was one of the best desserts I had had, and unlike in India where most of the desserts had an overdose of sugar, here one could feel the play of texture and temperature with the crumbly and warm cake and the creamy and cold gelato. The sweetness was there, but like background music, allowing other flavours to play their part.

When I turned my attention to Baba, his food rested untouched and there were three empty miniatures next to it. I knew that from now on I was to live the life of a working single mother, many of whom had inspired me through their podcasts.

When we landed, the experience was at odds with my imagination of what London would be. I was hoping to leave the airport gates and be greeted by the Big Ben, the London Eye and the white dome—all standing together within a single view. But after an instant swab test, we left the airport to take the underground metro, which Ben kept calling 'the tube'. A hoard of people descended upon the train and our oversized luggage did not make matters any easier.

After forty-five minutes of being in congested tunnels, we

finally saw a side of London that attested my imagination. The Trafalgar Square stood as a beating personification of what London meant to people who had never been there. It was evening, and in one magic moment, the Christmas tree in front of us lit up just as we ascended from the stairs. The dome of the gallery against the sky with its hues of violet, as if it was ablaze with hope, the fountain with those brooding bronze lions, hundreds of people dressed in overcoats and caps, a band of musicians playing carols, parents strolling with their children or dogs in prams, and street performers trying to get the fleeting attention of travellers—this was what dreams looked like if they were to come true.

'Let's go! You have you to check in,' Ben was yelling. I looked at him and then my heart sank. Baba was nowhere to be seen!

'Ben! Where's Baba?' I asked in sheer panic and we started looking for him in a frenzy. What seemed like the best dream to be in, had rapidly transformed into the worst nightmare to be trapped in. I started clutching at every old man in a chequered blazer and turning them around; my Baba was nowhere to be found. I was sobbing, telling myself that there had always been something ominous to this offer from the start. Not knowing what to do or where to go, I hoped that soon I would wake up in my bed in Himachal and resume that familiar life.

'Sita! Sita!' Ben was shouting from a distance. I rushed towards him. Baba was standing in front of a crowd, he was keenly watching a stout Middle-eastern man who was playing a shell game by hiding a stone under three identical wooden cups. His counterpart, a lean man in a green sweater, was taking people's bets. Baba took out a rolled bundle of pounds from his under pocket and put it in the lanky man's baggy cap. We were afar, rushing towards him, but Baba could not see us; he pointed at the middle cup, the chubby man uncovered that cup and there was nothing, nothing underneath the cup and nothing in our pockets.

'Up the sprout!' Ben remarked. I tore through the crowd and grabbed Baba by his hand. At that moment, the lost money did not matter. I was just relieved to find Baba. He was sheepishly guilty for his childish impulse. London had truly given me a welcome to remember.

I slept well past noon but there was no way to tell. It was a break day before I began work at the restaurant. The quarantine measures had recently been lifted for vaccinated travellers, which meant we could go and see the city. I opened the connecting door leading to the other room; Baba too had just woken up. All the travellers who had come to our café used to complain of jet-lag and back then I was unable to understand what it felt like, but today I could experience it first-hand. Poor Baba, he was not even aware of what he was suffering from.

We had the day to ourselves and after a late breakfast, we decided to head out. While dressing, I looked up multiple styles on Pinterest, TikTok and Instagram. I paired my beige overcoat, which I had picked up from the Mall Road, with oversized black corduroys, which I had been wearing for the past five years. I accessorised this with a red bean cap and a chequered muffler. I was never much into fashion but now being abroad, I felt a certain obligation to look my best. The look I selected on Instagram did not display a corduroy pant but blue jeans. In my village, unmarried girls were tagged indecent if they wore jeans, especially well fitted ones. Wearing jeans, sitting pillion on a bike which did not belong to your father or brother, driving a car if one could afford it and watching English movies—all these activities would immediately brand a girl as 'fast or modern' in our district.

'Lipstick? I don't have a nude shade! Do I have time for nail polish? What's the point? I'll be wearing gloves for the most part. I shouldn't have saved money and picked up those jeans and boots! Let's just wear sports shoes, they're comfortable!' These scattered thoughts ran through my head as I finished dressing up. Baba too was ready and we headed to the lift.

'Two all-day travel passes please,' I asked the receptionist while looking at the brochure for travellers.

'Ma'am, you have a chartered vehicle as a part of the package,' the receptionist confirmed. 'Your car will be here in five minutes,' he added. Whether Arun had thought of it or Ben, it was a considerate gesture to give us a car for the day.

And there we were, on the roads of London. I had hoped the car would navigate us effortlessly through these beautiful roads but we were stuck in unreasonably long traffic jams, and to make matters worse, next to us was a double-decker bus, barricading the views of the street.

'Sir, you can go back. We'll manage,' I told the driver. Baba and I stepped out and took the bus standing next to us. At first, the bus driver was reluctant to let us in; it was not a bus stop, but looking at our enthusiasm, he gave in. We rushed through the narrow stairs to reach the open upper deck which was relatively empty with just an old English couple and a few Asian boys similar to me in age, their bags and identity cards gave away that they were students.

The bus drove through the Regent Street on to Piccadilly Circus. Baba was animated like a schoolboy upon seeing such vibrant LEDs and marvellous Victorian buildings, but he still was not able to come to terms with the idea of being abroad. In our psyche, it was a right reserved for the rich and was well beyond our aspirations and imagination.

I was crushingly disappointed when I saw the Big Ben in a burqa—covered from the sight of strangers due to some prolonged restoration work.

I was constantly on my mobile, reading about the places we were seeing. *'Is it even worth coming to London if you don't hear the Big Ben chime, see it in all its glory and click a selfie with the clock tower in the background?'* I wondered. Baba was living the moment, capturing every image through his eyes and not his phone, savouring everything for himself and not his followers. We crossed over the Thames via the Westminster Bridge and entered a residential neighbourhood. A couple of red lights later, I instinctively felt that we should not go beyond. Baba and I hopped off the bus to enter a Turkish kebab joint. I ordered a chicken doner kebab, which Baba and I split in two.

'Fifteen Hundred Rupees for a doner roll!' I reacted upon seeing the price list and after doing a quick currency conversion in my head. As a part of the job, we had got a relocation allowance, most of which Baba had gambled away last evening, but thankfully I had kept a small sum with me.

We walked through the unknown streets and neighbourhoods of London, clicking multiple selfies and every once in a while, asking a passer-by to click us while we posed like tourists who used to do similar things at our café. We walked along the Thames; it was terribly cold on the bank but the riverside was soothing to the eyes. We both were craving tea but I ordered only one cup; I could make another when

I was back in the room. The sun was about to set when we took a bus back to our hotel at The Oxford Circus. Standing in the corridor, right before we parted ways for our respective rooms, Baba turned to me and placed his hand on my cheek, his eyes welled up and he leaned forward to kiss my forehead.

It was 5 a.m. when I turned off the television and 7 a.m. when the alarm rang. Today was the big day, a day I did not even know I had always dreamt of in the dimly lit depths of my subconscious. My reporting was at eleven and Ben said he would see me at the reception at 10:15 a.m.

I took a shower, wore my salwaar-kameez with a warmer underneath and a cardigan and an overcoat on top; London was too cold for a city in the plains. Baba and I stepped down for breakfast, we barely spoke and ate our food in a hurry to keep time at hand.

'Have your medicines, eat on time and don't go out alone,' I signed. At first, he resisted, but then agreed to my requests. We got up and he hugged me tightly and then he took out a red thread and tied it around my wrist. The onlookers were looking at us suspiciously, but neither Baba nor I could care less. It was a mauli, a sacred thread tied around the wrist for protection against evil and danger.

Those few steps from our table to the doorway in the dining hall felt like walking through a quicksand of time. With each step I was leaving my Baba behind and venturing into a world of my choosing. From the threshold opening into the lobby, I waved at him and turned around to greet Ben who was waiting at the reception.

'Am I late?' I asked.

'No, darling. The restaurant business is not for the early birds, not unless you bake bread,' Ben said while taking his teal overcoat and hat from the hat stand and we headed out into the streets of London.

'We'll find you accommodation this month,' he said as we walked past a flurry of people getting out of the tube station and heading to work. My dreams of taking a leisurely walk in the sun were transformed into a fidgety trot against the crowd with sheets of icy wind slapping my cheeks. From the circus we walked on to Regent Street and at the junction of Regent and Maddox, a black canopy arched over the facade of an ivory-coloured Victorian building; its canvas read 'Bellissimo' in cursive.

'Since it's your first day, take the main door, but remember rule number one—the staff must always use the service door,' Ben said. A cold gloom resided in the dark and empty dining room. It was difficult to imagine that soon this place would be brimming with life. As we entered the kitchen Ben held my hand and said, 'The second rule number one—always wear a cap in the kitchen,' he reached out for a cotton sleeve hanging on a hook. It was full of single use caps; he wore his and gave one to me.

'Good morning, everyone,' Ben called out to a rather busy dozen. It was my first time inside a kitchen of this scale. Though the floor was huge, it looked congested with vessels of varying sizes, steel partitions and platforms. Each person was at their designated station, working with a certain precision. I could not help but wonder, *'Where do I fit in this clockwork?'*

Under an array of LED tubes, two chefs were tirelessly chopping and blending heaps of tomatoes and garlic. The aprons and chef coats worn by the crew were indicative of their ranks, the senior-looking staff had coats with black buttons studded like medals of bravery, and the ones in plain white aprons had the humility of a foot soldier. Though they all wore different coats and headgear, the shoes were alike—black, broad, gender agnostic shoes marching on the tiled floor.

'Move!' A young chef screeched as he dashed across the pathway towards the giant refrigerator with a tray of lusciously layered Tiramisu.

'Did I tell you we make our own desserts and bread, unlike most restaurants who outsource the desserts and sometimes even the bread,' Ben said and I just gave a short, courteous smile. I was completely enchanted by the chaos of the kitchen.

'Good morning! Everyone, we have our new colleague all the way from India!' Ben yelled again and this time everyone stopped and took notice.

'Meet Sita Pandit, the chef Arun has been talking about,' he announced and it occurred to me that Arun had not met us since we had come to London; while we were planning to move, he would routinely check in through Ben, but I don't think even Ben knew of his current whereabouts.

'Good, you have them lined up,' Arun came into the kitchen and said, as if he was reading my thoughts while waiting in the wings.

'Hope you had a comfortable journey,' he asked. I wanted to talk properly but I just smiled like one of the many timid schoolgirls I knew from back home. It was uncharacteristic of me to feel nervous.

'Let me introduce you to everyone,' he spoke warmly, trying to make up for his absence.

'Philip Gower, our restaurant manager,' Arun said, referring to an Englishman in his late fifties. The first thing one would notice about him was his large built—not strong but just large—his receding hairline and puffy eyes. I was conscious to not appear impolite and shifted my attention from his eyes while shaking hands.

'Welcome to Bellissimo, Miss Pandit, I hope we set you up for success,' said Philip in a cordial but monotonous tone, mispronouncing my second name and I didn't bother or felt informal enough to correct him.

'Beyond that door, it's his realm, the serving staff reports to him,' Ben interjected.

'What time do we open?' I asked and there was a moment of silence as if everyone expected me to know these meticulous details.

'Twelve to three in the afternoon and six to ten in the evening,' Ben replied. 'It's written on the porch,' he whispered and then introduced me to the next person. Arun, by now, had decided to divert his attention to matters in the kitchen, inspecting what was cooking on every live flame and what was written on the dozens of lists strung across a wall. He was keeping an eye on the back door from where vendors were delivering fresh vegetables.

'Meet our pastry chef, Dino Moretti,' Ben said, introducing the tall lean man who had swished past us with the Tiramisu.

'*Benvenuto a Londra*, Welcome to London,' he said with a twinkle in his blue eyes and a smile across that stubbly face. He was strikingly good looking, something I had noticed about most Italian men since many of them visited our café too. I did owe a large part of my cooking to those travellers; the books and the videos could only provide meticulous details on how to cook a particular dish but how does one know if it tastes authentic or not? And that is where our customers at The Midway Café helped me a great deal. I acknowledged Dino's gesture and Ben introduced me to the next person, a chubby blonde in her late twenties wearing a white crumpled chef's coat. It was not difficult to tell that she did most of the heavy lifting in the kitchen.

'She's Alice, the sous chef at Bellissimo,' he said. I offered a handshake but she put on a rather phoney smile and showed her dough-coated hands.

'I hope you like it here,' she said and then she headed back to her station, where she was kneading and flattening dough.

'Is that a pasta maker?' I asked in amazement, referring to a steel machine on the counter, similar to the ones I had seen in many videos.

'Yes, sweetheart,' she spoke sweetly but with an obvious disregard in her tone.

'Alice is assisted by Kathy, and our man, Jason, manages the grill; sauté chef, Ryan, he also does the sauces; and good old Tom is the roundsman—a jack of all trades you can say,' Ben said, introducing these four, all of whom were in their mid or late thirties. I could assess that they probably were not from a fancy culinary school but were battle-hardened in the confines of the kitchen. Jason was a giant teddy-bearish man, wearing his white chef coat and an apron stained with patches of red, rust and olive. Ryan was of African descent and appeared rather sophisticated. 'Welcome,' said Ryan. 'Take it easy on the first day, let us know if you need something,' Jason added. They both had pressing matters on the flame and returned to tend to them.

'Mario, late as usual, manages the seafood, cold cuts and pork,' Ben said, pointing at an empty butcher station.

'And these jolly folks are Chris and Nick, or Chris and Cross as we call them,' he said, referring to two boys no older than me; they were the ones who were diligently chopping

tomatoes and garlic on an industrial scale. Nick was a lanky
young lad with two piercings, baggy jeans, an apron, a faded
t-shirt and orangish curly hair peeking out of his cap, while
Chris was a muscle mountain with his hair neatly gelled back,
visible through his transparent cap.

'Welcome,' they both said in tandem. 'I love India, haven't
been there though. One day...' Nick expressed.

Ben gestured at me to walk with him to the far end of
the kitchen. Arun was talking to an old man who donned
a thick white beard with surma[24] in his eyes, wore a round
knitted white cap on his head and a leather apron with stains
of aged blood. He was aware of my presence but continued to
converse with Arun in a dialect which was a blend of Hindi,
Urdu and Punjabi. He took his butcher's knife and sharpened
it on the leather strop tied on the slab where his wooden log
was resting; though his eyes were locked in a conversation
with Arun, his hands were flawlessly moving through a pile
of meat on the log, shifting from one end of the stack to
another; and then he flipped the meat around and repeated
the same rhythmic chops.

'Sita, meet Anwar Khan, our very own Khan Chacha. He
does with a butcher's knife what Bernini did with a chisel,'
Arun introduced us.

'Bernini?' I asked.

'Never mind,' he said. I folded my hands and greeted
the old man who nodded reservedly before going back to
mincing the meat.

'Here, take this,' Arun said, tossing a white chef's coat
at me. It was at least two sizes big for me.

---

[24]Surma: Kohl

'Call Harvey & Sons. Get her's stitched,' Arun instructed Ben. From the back door entered a woman in a charcoal-coloured chef's coat, fitting well around her lean but hardy frame. No older than thirty, 'GR' were the initials on her pocket and the coat was a couple of inches shorter than the usual length of a chef's coat. Looking at her jacket, one would be convinced that this was the perfect length and everyone else was wearing it wrong all along. She strutted past us in her tight black jeans, effortlessly owned her short blonde hair, nose piercing and mascara. She then put on her black chef's hat, which again was a customised one, resembling a soldier's cap worn sideways—a beret; I googled it later.

'My grandma is eighty and has cataracts, even she can chop finer than this!' She reprimanded Nick who was chopping the garlic rather unevenly. I had heard from multiple Italian chefs that the finer the garlic is chopped, the more flavour it imparts. She had a fair complexion, multiple piercings in her ears, a nose ring and a tattoo on the back of her neck, which was half visible from beneath the collar of her coat. She looked like a girl a lot of boys would chase unsuccessfully. I had never seen or met a woman like her; I thought only men could be this assertive in what they do.

'Bucatini, Linguine and Penne, al dente[25],' she ordered.

'Yes, Chef!' said Alice. The woman then went to the refrigerator and carved a small square from the Tiramisu.

'From tomorrow, spike up the marsala and sprinkle some cinnamon and nutmeg in too. This'll be a part of the Christmas set menu,' she told Dino who nodded submissively.

---

[25]Al Dente: A way of cooking pasta or rice so it remains slightly firm with a bite.

'Phil, tell the boys to come at eleven from tomorrow and no offs this month. Christmas time is business time,' she instructed Philip.

'Yes, Chef!' he said. She walked over to the lists hanging on the wall and took a pen from her arm pocket and started making alterations to them. I stood mesmerised, looking at this woman who ruled this kitchen like a queen.

'Come,' said Arun and we walked across to the wall plastered with paper.

'Gabby,' he said. She took a few good seconds to finish what she was writing before turning her attention to Arun.

'Meet Sita, the one I was telling you about,'

'Your Himalayan wonder?' She asked. Whether she was matter of fact or condescending, I could not tell.

'Welcome,' she said rather indifferently.

'Just observe for the first week. Alice will help you find you a place,' she said, making a fleeting eye contact with Alice.

'She can hit the ground running, let me show you,' Arun interjected.

'Sita, could you make that Himalayan Aglio Olio please?' Arun asked me. 'We have flown in the Kashmiri Gucchi,' he added.

'Sure,' I said. I could be sleepwalking and I would still get this one dish right. I walked to a station, took a saucepan and put some water in it. I looked at the burner and that's when it struck me that this was not my café—the familiarity and comfort of my own kitchen was amiss. I tried to light the stove but the pilot was different from the stove I had at home. I gave it another shot; it did not turn on. Thankfully, one of the chefs—Chris or Nick, I forgot which was who— came forward and lit it. I put the water filled pan to boil and added a fist's width worth of spaghetti. As the pasta was put to boil, I turned my attention to the garlic.

'Work with these,' Gabby said, keeping the chopped garlic aside and handing me a fresh bulb.

'What are you doing?' Alice asked when she saw me dip the unpeeled pods in water so they could lose the skin easily.

'To peel ...' I said, choking with self-doubt.

'That's one way to do it, or you can just pinch the bud at its nip. Don't worry, that's not what we have you here for—not to peel garlic, I hope,' Gabby said and Alice giggled. This demo was slowly turning into a test. Everyone converged near the station but Arun stood at a distance, observing the proceedings. I managed to peel the garlic, stopping at six buds; then it was time to chop. I was becoming increasingly conscious to not be corrected for uneven chopping. I was trying to slice the garlic so fine it was almost paper-like. During those first few chops, my hands and knees were trembling involuntarily. Even though my eyes were on the chopping board, my mind was focused on the eyes upon me. The first two cloves went fine and just when I eased my attention a bit, the knife sliced through the skin near my index fingernail and the entire bud turned red.

'Ice water!' Ryan yelled and a helper in the kitchen dashed towards us with a bowl of water. I dipped my finger in it, watching my blood slowly dissolve in the cup. Chris and Nick came with a Band-aid.

I had made a fool of myself and perhaps of Arun too.

Amid all this, the boiling water started to spill out of the pan, making the flames beneath run astray. In a split second, the butter greased morels, which I had kept on the side, caught fire and the flames became violently high. Jason rushed in with a small extinguisher to douse it. It had all become a great mess, a mess of which I was the highlight. Some people were concerned about me but Alice had no qualms about hiding her amusement. Arun looked at my finger, which was now being dressed.

'It's not deep, will heal in a matter of hours. Tend to the wound today and come back fresh tomorrow,' he said.

'What a waste of those air flown morels!' Gabby taunted in a tone low enough so not everyone could hear, but firm enough that Arun and I could.

'All right folks, back to your stations,' she said loudly and everyone dispersed to do their impending tasks while I stood with my self-respect extinguished by humiliation.

'Did I let him down? Was this all a mistake? Is this beyond me?' The thoughts flowed through my head while I waited for the blood to stop flowing.

5

U-Turn

Sita

'*She can't even be a dishwasher. Prude! Who let her on a plane, she doesn't deserve to be here ...*'

I woke up with my back soaked in sweat; the voices in my head still lingering on.

'*Was it all a dream?*' I thought, but the Band-aid on my left index finger conjured the embarrassment from yesterday. I lay in bed motionless, staring at the ceiling. This feeling of internal discomposure reminded me of the time when I lost Ma; I was ten then and perhaps, the naivety of childhood was the antidote to that insurmountable feeling of loss. But today, this gloom was darker and deeper, I felt crippled by my inability to frame thoughts and struggled to find a reason to get up and start my day. The paint on the walls didn't change, but they appeared a few shades darker. It was sunny outside but I only saw charcoal grey clouds. I closed my eyes and pictured myself in my village, standing in my kitchen garden after a bath and bathing in the warmth of the winter sun;

nostalgia is a blanket woven with memories once mundane. I wasted half an hour in that state of inertia, replaying the events from yesterday and dreading the ones I would face today. Then, in a sudden jolt of impulsivity, I thrusted myself out of the bed and went straight into the shower, hoping that the hot water would wash away the humiliation.

At breakfast, I forced myself through a bowl of fruits so Baba would not get anxious. I put on a facade of being excited about my work, when in reality, I was standing under a waterfall of self-doubt. The streets of London, which had enticed me so far, had also lost their freshness like a bouquet of flowers on the fourth day. I crossed the main door of the restaurant and turned left into a narrow alley leading to the service door. I stopped afar, like a thief would, upon seeing the police; Alice, Gabby and Dino were standing at the far end of the alley in front of the back door, smoking their cigarettes and talking animatedly.

'*Are they mocking me?*' I wondered, hiding behind a car, trying not to catch their sight. The thought of taking the front door did occur and I almost convinced myself, but then I remembered rule number one. Staying put, I peeped from behind the car; they were still there, now with fresh cigarettes in their hands. I stooped a little to remain concealed, and in an effort to pass time, I kept finding new visual diversions. Paint chipping off the walls, window panes with broken glass, the odd leak in the plumbing and the stench of sewer—the back alley was in stark contrast to the manicured main streets.

'*I can't be hiding like a sheep,*' I thought and mustered myself out of this fear, paced through those dreaded yards and crossed my colleagues without a morning greeting from either side.

'She has the gall to show up!' Alice commented.

'Don't worry, her days are numbered,' taunted Gabby, aware that I was in audible distance.

In the kitchen, all the chefs were going about their chores, often staring at me from a distance or giving that cosmetic good morning nod if our paths crossed. Arun and Ben were nowhere to be seen, and while everyone on the floor was driven by their job, I was finding it unsettling to not have a direction to follow.

'Good you are here. Hope that finger is fine,' said Alice with a disdain that was hard to miss. Gabby also came, reeking of cigarettes and went straight past me to Khan Chacha and the other butcher—'Mario' I recalled. Their body language during the conversation looked like what they were discussing was more important than anything else happening on the floor, much like a village panchayat[26] assembled together while we stood like a collective crowd, which individually lacked an identity and a voice. Alice and her brigade of station chefs were working with a pressing sense of urgency; sounds of knives cutting through different textures, ranging from fresh and crunchy vegetables to soft-boiled potatoes, blenders running at top speed where at first their advance is met with resistance by the ingredients, but within seconds everything becomes a smooth liquidy blend. The cross-station-shouting by the chefs and the occasional banter and laughter filled the room—even the clock hanging on the wall had better purpose than I did.

Philip entered from the door leading to the dining hall. 'We open in fifteen,' he shouted and left and the sense of urgency, which already gripped everyone, suddenly turned into

---

[26]Panchayat: A system of governance in villages

panic. The actions grew faster and the shouting louder.

'That pig will graduate by the time you carve it!' Gabby yelled at Mario.

'I don't need to tell you on a daily basis! Put that damn pasta to boil,' she reprimanded Alice and Kathy. The latter immediately put three saucepans of varying sizes on the stove. From whatever little I had known of Kathy, one thing I knew for sure was that she was being bullied in her job; her constant fear of being pulled up was visible in her actions.

'Bread baskets?' Gabby asked Dino as she continued marching down the kitchen aisle.

'Yes, Chef,' Dino responded while he prepared an array of similar looking bread baskets to offer to the customers as they waited for their orders. Most of the things which were happening in this kitchen, I could relate them to the cooking and kitchen videos I had seen.

'You're still here?' Gabby asked, I was caught off guard.

'Come on! Let's get you some work. Chris, Nick, get her to assist you,' she said, enlisting me in the ancillary staff working on the peripheral tasks of the kitchen. Nick hesitated, not knowing what work to assign me; they both were commies in the kitchen, the junior-most chefs, fresh out of a culinary school and the only people below them in the hierarchy were the dishwashing and housekeeping staff. Now, I too was on that list.

'Here,' said Chris, handing me a white apron.

'I guess you can peel and chop the garlic?' Nick said and then his expressions revealed that he remembered what had happened yesterday.

'Actually, don't worry. Why don't you focus on peeling and I'll chop? We'll finish fast,' he said and at that point there was nothing I could say or do. Yesterday I had my chance to shine and I made a mess of it.

The clock hit eleven and a bell rang in the kitchen; it was not a blaring alarm but a subdued buzzer that everyone on the floor could hear.

'We're open for business!' Chris said, standing between two baskets full of whole and chopped tomatoes, his hands were working like a machine, it reminded me of Chotu in my own kitchen.

'In the hours before business, focus on the preparation. Potatoes—we boil first and then peel unless the chef asks otherwise, tomatoes—you can never have enough chopped and pureed tomatoes with you, they are used in most of the bases we do. Then come the mushrooms, tiny sons of guns— they take up all the time in cleaning and chopping, but when you expose them to heat, their volume reduces like a pay-check after taxes. And there's basil, cashews and pine nuts for the pesto. Last, but not the least, we have our friend—the garlic, the king of flavour. Ryan, the sauté chef takes most of what we do and Alice looks after the cheese herself. Be alert, we get shoutouts whenever a salad is ordered. Ajmal here is a smart lad, he keeps the greens washed and fresh so they don't look like they are straight out of the fridge. And don't worry about the tossing, Kathy does the garde manger[27] assemblies,' Nick explained earnestly and Ajmal, who was slightly younger than us, smiled to introduce himself before being summoned by Alice to fetch something from the refrigerator.

For the first half an hour since opening, nothing dramatic happened. The chefs continued their preparation and I peeled

---

[27]Garde Manger: A 'cold' station for salads and uncooked appetisers

one garlic bud after another. By 11.45 a.m. we could hear murmurs from outside and a fancy looking LED board in the kitchen, with numbers from one to thirty, lit up with numbers 3, 5 and 11 in red.

'That's Arun's ingenuity. We know which tables are occupied and which are empty even before the orders reach us,' Chris said while washing his hands in the basin.

'It's an easy midweek afternoon. We'll host a few dandy housewives, the servers bear with their chatter, and we also get the odd banker or lawyer who come here for their meetings over a pint. The evenings get quite busy though, and come Friday until the Sunday brunch, you will practically live here,' he added. I listened to him while observing Gabby, she was constantly referring to a giant screen where the orders came as notifications and she, in turn, was instructing her squadron of chefs. She moved effortlessly from one station to the other, knowing exactly where and when she was needed. She did the final plating on all the dishes and sporadically tasted the various sauces which were on the simmer. Jason was roasting the meats, being constantly supplied by both the butchers.

'Khan Chacha is the eldest,' Nick said, pronouncing 'chacha' rather oddly.

'You all call him Chacha?' I was curious to know why so many foreigners called him 'chacha'.

'Yeah, actually Arun does and we all just followed. He was the first one to start Bellissimo with Arun. It was him, Arun and Anthony.'

'Anthony?' I asked and 'Shushh…' he hushed me, signaling convolutedly. And then Chris took a step closer and started to whisper.

'Anthony Dellucci, our executive chef. It was like a

movie. Arun was the producer, but Anthony the director. It was his food that pulled people in. They both worked like a couple—Arun's vision and Anthony's skill made Bellissimo one of the most sought-after Italian restaurants here. Before the pandemic, we even had a wait list running into weeks.

'We managed to live through the crisis when most could not, but then, Anthony wanted to have his name on the porch—"Bellissimo by Anthony Dellucci"—he wanted us rechristened,' said Nick.

'Arun refused and they both had a showdown right here in the kitchen. And that was the end of the old Bellissimo. Things have not been the same since then. The local food guides and bloggers covered Anthony's departure extensively and it was only a matter of time before he came up with his own restaurant,' he explained.

'That too just a throw away from here, at The Wardour,' Chris chipped in.

'Teatro by Anthony Dellucci, it's called. A homage to the film scene on that street,' he added. None of it made sense to me as he was explaining it, but later, I searched for 'Anthony Dellucci, Wardour and Teatro.' Anthony was an Italian chef who had spent two decades in London; first working at The Claridge's and then, starting Bellissimo. He was also extremely popular on Instagram and was recognised for his modern take on authentic Italian dishes, like Lamb Kidney with Anchovies, Vegan Pesto Pizza, Guanciale[28] with bell peppers and a host of Sardinian dishes. Wardour was a street in Westminster and Teatro meant theatre.

'You know the critics and the rich dig that stuff. I mean,

---

[28]Guanciale: An Italian dish with cured pork cheeks

the food he serves is no different than ours, but his investor got an agency to conceptualise the theme of the restaurant and that was just the kind of recognition Anthony was after,' Nick said.

'They even approached us for a job, but Ben outsmarted them. He gave everyone in the kitchen a pay hike with a two-year lock in and no compete.' He added.

'Thank god for Gabby! By designation, she is also a sous chef like Alice, but she was Anthony's understudy and the moment Anthony stepped out, she rose to the occasion. He walked away on a Friday afternoon. We could have been shut for weeks, but thanks to her, not a single dish was delayed,' Chris said.

'She is due for a promotion. I think Arun will make her the executive chef,' he added.

'He better. We can't afford for her to be poached from here,' replied Nick.

'Take the inventories, will you?' Gabby approached and ordered, handing me a printed list. I was rendered clueless. Chris was standing opposite me and behind Gabby's back, he pointed me in the direction of the service door where a vendor truck had come and they were unloading fruits and vegetables.

I went to the door; two Turkish men were unloading the fresh produce at lightning-fast pace. There were bundles of lettuce, sacks of ginger and garlic, smaller packets of micro greens and basil, and what felt like a town's supply of potatoes, tomatoes and yellow onions. One man approached me with a list, asking for my signature and I signed, they sat in their mini-truck and left as swiftly as they had appeared. Receiving customers from all over the world at my café, I had developed a knack for identifying people's nationality by their appearance or accent.

Gabby, Alice and Dino came to the threshold. Gabby and Dino stepped out to light a cigarette and Alice asked me to show her the list Gabby had given me.

'What's this?' she asked.

'The list...' I spoke timidly.

'I know genius. Why the hell is it empty?' she yelled.

'I am sorry...' I tried to offer an explanation but she turned away. Gabby was observing all this.

'How thick are these people?' she said to Gabby.

'Ajmal, come here and list down the inventory,' said Gabby.

'Oh daddy, this little Himalayan flower wants to be a star chef,' Alice acted in jest.

'Yeah baby, feed me that nectar and daddy bee will make you the best chef ever,' mocked Gabby, taking part in this vulgar pantomime.

'Oh, come on daddy bee, sting me, sting me hard!' she enticed Dino.

'Hahahaha!'

They all broke out in laughter and I too broke out in inconsolable tears and rushed to the restroom.

Ben

'Christmas in Disneyland and Gstaad for New Year?' Arun proposed to Amira, his ten-year-old daughter. We were driving to her mother's house in Richmond after picking her up from school. When I started working for Arun, he also lived there, but within months, he and Natasha had an amicable separation after ten years of marriage, and as a part of the settlement, she got to keep the house and the child. From whatever little he revealed to me, I could gather that his relentless hours at work and an incurable inclination towards other women caused the two to part ways, though he maintains he never slept with another woman while he was married. After the separation, instead of moving back with his parents, Arun moved into a lavish bachelor pad at Mayfair, fully devoting himself to the two reasons that led to his separation in the first place.

'No, Pa! Ma made her plans with me two months ago!' said Amira. In appearance, she took after her mother, but had a temperament to match her father's. As a child who also saw his parents separate, I always felt that children who go through that, grow beyond their years. She was all but ten and her mannerisms were already that of a teenager—keeping to herself for the most part and by herself, I mean, her phone screen, and giving a default 'no' for an answer to most of the things her parents would propose. Arun was known to have his way with people, either through the sorcery of his words or his bullish persistence, but that seldom worked with Amira. The drive from the school to her home was rather short and soon, we were outside the beautiful three-storey landed house, which still bore Arun's name on the plate.

'Are you sure?' he asked.

'Yes, Pa. Don't make me say no,'

'Then don't'

'You're impossible. See you,' she hugged her father from the passenger seat and got out of the car.

Natasha came out to the front lawn and with her was Diljeet Maan, a brooding six-feet-four Sikh who was an ex-rugby player of local repute. In his ivory wool chesterfield coat and turban, dark blue denims and brown boots, he was nothing short of a modern knight. Amira went and hugged her mother, who in turn gave a kiss on her forehead; from the distance, it all looked like a life insurance commercial on television. Well into her late thirties, Natasha carried herself with the flawless grace of a proper lady, but with those close to her, she had a wit like a sailor. And beyond that veneer of wit and grace, there was a woman of grit, a woman who did not think twice before showing Arun the door. Like Arun, she too grew up in London in a family of immigrants, but unlike her ex-husband, she strived to find a balance in her life—a balance between professional and personal and between parenting and love. She reminded me of the image of an Indian goddess where a woman would balance multiple things in her multiple hands. A human resource consultant with Barclays, Natasha also helped Arun in the formative years of Bellissimo to truly make it a fine-dining gourmet experience when it could have well been limited to a pseudo-Italian takeaway joint. From the car, Arun was watching his wife and daughter together, and he too was witnessing his ex-wife's appeal. Then Amira hugged Diljeet, not a parental hug which oozes affection but more like a warm greeting. He patted her on the back and the two conversed for a brief moment before Amira went inside the house. The car was too small to contain Arun's rage, and his ex-wife's steady boyfriend for two-and-a-half years had also spotted us. Arun now had no option but to go out and put on a social farce in an effort to be 'the better man.'

Diljeet greeted us with a handshake, his giant palms

engulfed Arun's and when he shook mine, I was awestruck by the sheer manliness of this dark and brooding hunk. Arun had the sophistication of a gilded ceremonial sword, but Diljeet was forged like a cast iron battle-axe; they both had their occasions to wield.

'Join us for lunch,' he said, inviting Arun to his own home. Had he not been this horse of a man, I am sure Arun would have slapped him. His 'better man' charade gave in; he went straight to Natasha and the two were talking incandescently—I would call it borderline fighting—and after a brief confrontation, Arun left fuming as always. I followed. We were back on the road again and Arun, who usually is a calm driver, drove like Bhaiya from Shimla.

We reached the restaurant and dashed in through the back door; the first thing Arun saw was Sita standing at the most insignificant corner of the kitchen, peeling garlic.

'Goddammit, have I got you all the way from India to peel garlic? Is that all you got? Why do you even bother showing up then?' Arun blasted Sita off, throwing a fist full of garlic against the wall. She stood there, stunned, shivering and sobbing. Everyone else stopped working and looked at Arun, they were used to his outbursts, which didn't become less petrifying with time. It did not matter if you were at the receiving end or were just a spectator, his rage would linger beyond his words. Arun left for his office and everyone else, including Sita, stood still; her hands were trembling, eyes and nose flowing and before I could approach her, she ran out through the backdoor.

❧

Ben

'When did they leave?' I asked over the phone.

'Twenty minutes ago,' replied the hotel receptionist. I urged our Hackney driver to drive fast, an impossibility on the roads of London. Thankfully, we reached in time. Sita and Hira Lal were placing their luggage on the trolley when I intercepted them at the departure gate at Heathrow. She saw me and swiftly walked past; I rushed back, barricading her advance.

'You can't leave!' I asserted.

'Let me go, Ben,' she said, still sobbing and trying to dodge me to find a way through. I looked at Hira, inciting him to intervene and stop his daughter; with hesitation, he made a failed attempt.

'What time is your flight beta?' Khan Chacha stepped forward and asked, he had accompanied me to the airport. *'Stop the girl before she does something silly,'* he had told me in the kitchen in his customary reserved demeanour when Sita left after being lambasted by Arun.

'10 p.m.,' she said.

'There is time, have a cup of tea with me,' he said and though reluctant, she agreed to his request. We found a cosy spot inside a Starbucks brimming with passengers. We ordered our drinks and in spite of the background chatter, there was an awful silence at our table, breached intermittently by Hira slurping his piping hot tea.

'How is my Hindustan?' Khan Chacha asked and Sita, who was looking outside the window so far, was now forced to engage in a conversation. Khan Chacha had that effect on people, his appearance was rather intimidating but his tongue so polite that one would fear him yet respect him for how he treated you.

'It's not perfect, but it's home. Are you from India?' she asked.

'I don't know, beta. It's been twenty years since I last visited. Here, I will never become one of these gora[29] sahebs and back home, I feel like an outsider,' Khan Chacha said. His thick veins were jutting through his muscular arms and hands, his wrinkled forehead, deep eyes and long white beard were like a leather-bound memoir.

'Where are you from?' Sita asked.

'Abba was from Layallpur. During the partition we moved to Sirhind and after many attempts, he moved to London in the seventies, I was ten then,' Khan Chacha said. In my three years of being at Bellissimo, this was the first time I had heard him open up about his roots.

'Your baba, he is proud of you. A father can see it in another father's eyes'.

'Thank you,' she said. 'You have children?'

'Three. The eldest, Sameena, is married to a chemist in Southall. Fatima, the middle one, works at a beauty parlour and Harun, our *sahabzada*, will join me soon,' Khan Chacha said. It did not surprise me that his son would follow in his footsteps to be a butcher. Arun had told me that Khan Chacha came from a lineage of butchers who had mastered their craft.

'They're afraid of you,' he spoke softly. 'When Arun came back from India, he would not stop talking about your skill, how you have a magic with flavours and pairings, which chefs take decades to master—"*Shafa aur barkat hai uske haathon me*[30]"—

---

[29]Gora: A Hindi slag for Caucasians
[30]Hindi for: You are a gifted chef

were his words to me,' Chacha said and Sita broke down. This was the first time that she had had a proper conversation with anyone since she moved; London can be overwhelming and it certainly had thrown her out of her element.

'Please don't ... you saw what happened. I am not meant for this ...'

'It is nothing but perseverance that lets a river cut through a mountain. I have spent my entire life in the restaurant business and if my eyes are not wronging me, you have what it takes to make it big,' he assured her. But she was not convinced.

'Success takes everything from you before it gives anything back. You have the gift, you need to learn the skill,' he added. Khan Chacha's pronunciation was coloured but he was a natural orator. Though he seldom spoke, the way he paused, stressed on the syllables and used his body to compliment his words, he created a profound impact on his listeners.

'And don't take his words to heart,' he said, defending Arun's outburst. 'His ways can be harsh but he means well. Arun too has seen failure before he became who he is,' Khan Chacha revealed, taking a big slurp from his milk-laden tea. He then waited for a moment to gauge an inquisitive cue from Sita; and on point, the sign came.

'He was a regular at The Claridge's where I was the butcher. He would spot even the most minor inconsistencies in the meat, the cut or the cooking. His taste and curiosity impressed me and over time, we became friends,' said Khan Chacha, recollecting a story Arun had told me more than a couple of times. Arun was a twenty-eight-year-old heir to the hundred-and-nine-year-old business, The Old Delhi Perfumery, which had a shop each at Dariba Kalan in Old

Delhi, Rue de Rivoli in Paris and here at Oxford Street in London. The family made their fortunes in pre-independent India by supplying musk, oud and other fragrances to the high-ranking British officials and exporting it for the English royalty. During his grandfather's time, the family migrated here and set up shops in London and Paris, eventually becoming a supplier of base fragrances to some of the most popular perfume labels worldwide. Arun was expected to take this business further, which for five generations prior to him was managed by the men of the Mehra family. Further he did take it, but not without earning disappointment from his father. Arun sold the majority share of the family business to a multinational who took their finances to new heights but in a direction opposite to his father's wishes.

'Arun had a family business to inherit, a princely life one would think, but his calling was elsewhere, his heart was in the restaurant business. And unlike you, he isn't a chef. In fact, he is the most horrible cook I've seen. But what he is, is a great connoisseur of food and a patron of chefs,' Khan Chacha told Sita. When Arun was young, he was influenced by his grandmother, Leela Mehra. She loved hosting elite Londoners over fancy high teas for an opportunity to boast her baking skills. For a young Arun, those post-school hours with his grandmother turned into a wonderland where according to him, his grandmother would *"routinely transform an unassuming tin of plain white flour, eggs and butter into extravagant pastries, pies, cakes and biscuits …"*

By the time Arun finished his schooling, obtaining a college degree was seen as a mere social obligation by his family and there were no pressures to inherit the family business; it was perceived as a certainty like the sun is expected to rise every morning. On a prolonged backpacking trip to Italy during his gap year, Arun fell in love with their music, architecture and food. Most of that year he spent travelling through the length of the country and serving part-time as the waiting staff of various restaurants. Upon his return, the young Arun could not muster the courage to stand up to his father—he went to college, following the course set out for him and then, he joined the family business. But soon, unbearable pangs of monotony set in. It was at The Claridge's that Arun met Khan Chacha and Anthony; Anthony Dellucci was an upcoming Italian chef and Khan Chacha's mastery over meat was already the stuff of folklore among steak aficionados. Arun coaxed and hired both of them with the dream of starting a progressive Italian restaurant in the heart of London.

'Bellissimo struggled initially, for six months it ran losses and even though we all thought it had failed, Arun did not give up. Those days advertising was expensive and he chose to spend every penny he had on curating the experience for his customers,' Khan Chacha said. '"*In the age of dubstep, we are playing a piano solo, give it time,*" Arun had told me after our doubts regarding the success of our venture,' Khan chacha explained and Sita looked at her phone discreetly, their boarding time was fast approaching.

'I clearly remember that afternoon. Arun was in his office, the rent and the salaries were overdue and he had no money left,' he added. One would think a man of Arun's fortune had a perennial well to dip his bucket in but his father was determined to make his venture fail. What happened next was a testimony to his resilience and ingenuity.

'"*I do not have any money to pay you or pay the rent,*" Arun told all of us. He then said that we had two options—to quit or use this kitchen to make box-meals which he would sell on the street to make ends meet. Some left, but most stayed, and for the next three months, we all worked extra shifts—serving gourmet meals to the one-off customers who came to the restaurant, but mostly to make spaghetti and penne in bulk. And Arun, he practically lived at the restaurant, working with the suppliers, the kitchen staff and then going out in a truck to sell boxed pasta outside stations and parks. He did what he had to keep the lights on,' said Khan Chacha.

'Word spread slowly, seekers of good food started coming to Bellissimo and soon, we were able to pay the rent, salaries and make a name for ourselves,' Khan Chacha recollected. By now, Sita was genuinely interested in his story.

'The quick-serve spaghetti became popular and as a memory of those times, Arun kept it on the menu as "Spaghetti in a box", which till date is our most sought-after dish,' Khan Chacha concluded.

'By telling this story, what I mean to tell you is—only those who endure the darkest hour get to see the first rays of light. Had Arun quit that day, his dream would have remained unfulfilled. And today, you have to think about your dream,' he asserted.

'Take it from this old man, food is your calling. And if you want to learn the ways of a professional kitchen, see me tomorrow at 7 a.m.,' he added and then we left, without an answer from Sita, without knowing if she would show up tomorrow or take her flight tonight.

6

The Grind

Sita

It was 5.50 a.m. I woke up ten minutes before the alarm. The room was dramatically lit for a sweeping moment by the headlamps of a car zooming past on the street below. While brushing my teeth, I stared into the blankness of the mirror, doubting if I had done the right thing by staying, thinking of going back home and not putting myself through the whims of an old man; the very next moment I brushed those thoughts aside. After my morning routine, I entered Baba's room; he was still asleep, I left him a text saying for the next few days I will leave for work early and he should go about his day as usual.

I stepped out of the hotel. It was still dark and drizzling after a night of heavy rain; I had to rely on Google Maps to guide me to the restaurant. I pulled the umbrella forward so the mobile would not get wet but in the process, my backpack did. Walking along the skirtings on the pavement, taking intermittent shelter under the canopies, I reached the restaurant at 6.50 a.m., Khan Chacha was in the kitchen, carving the meat; he signalled me to join him at the front station while he went to wash his hands. I put on an apron and a paper hat.

'Are you ready?' he asked and I nodded. Then he took a tabeez[31] and tied it around my arm, murmuring a prayer in Arabic.

'I will teach you the essentials of a professional kitchen, don't mistake them for tips. They will be your survival guide here,' he instructed and I took a deep breath, firming up my resolve.

'What does a restaurant mean to the customer? And what does a customer mean to a restaurant?' he asked as he paced through the narrow lane between the work stations. I did not have a response.

'From the moment a customer makes up his mind on what to order, you're against the clock and against their mounting expectations. In his head, the customer has already set a notion of how their dish will look, smell and taste. And this assumption is based on what he orders, from where and how much is he paying for it. The same grilled sandwich ordered at a 7 Eleven and a deli restaurant will get different reactions— even if the sandwich is exactly the same,' he said, though I was listening keenly, the image of a grilled sandwich did not help on a morning when I had missed my breakfast.

'A plate of the same Biryani for four pounds as opposed to twenty will taste different. Food that comes to your table in under ten minutes from ordering is thought to be tastier than orders which take more than twenty. Managing this part

---

[31]Tabeez: Amulet

of the restaurant business is what an executive chef and the restaurateur do together,' he explained.

'The easy thing about being a chef is to make delicious food, but the difficult part is to meet the customer's expectations consistently. You have to climb this mountain each day and there are no allowances for having a bad day. The quality of tomatoes is not the same? Too bad; the chef still has to make the same dish. Overbooked? It's not an excuse to serve something sloppy. Haven't had an off in two weeks? It doesn't matter to the person who is paying to eat your food!' he was yelling by the end of it.

'What he is saying makes sense, but what's with all the yelling?' I wondered.

'Cooking is one of the most consistent art forms. Footballers can have bad days, but not chefs, we don't have that margin. You will only be as good as your last meal, and if you are not where your customer expects you to be, you better pack your bags and go home!' he concluded while brimming with passion, something which I always had for food, but the last few days in the kitchen had jolted me.

'Now let's start with the basics—chopping. Cutting your ingredients at a fine dining restaurant is different from a regular eatery. The way a trained chef chops has a technique. Use your left knuckles above your nails as bastions while you hold the knife with your right. This will give your blade direction and stability and get you in a certain rhythm; but most importantly, it will protect your fingers,' he elaborated, demonstrating the chopping technique on a big white onion. At first, his hands were slow but then he started chopping with the momentum of the wheels of an express train. He was speeding through the onions, one after another, and within a minute there was a heap of finely and evenly chopped onions.

He brought his blade scarily close to my face. 'Remember, sharp knives cut food, blunt knives cut you,' he warned and handed me the knife, placing a basket full of tomatoes, onions, spinach, mint, eggplant and potatoes in front of me. At first, I was hesitant but he stood opposite me, showing me the circular motion with which the knife had to come down, how the blade would rest and brush against my knuckles and before I knew it, I was chopping in a seamless rhythm.

'Invest in a good knife set, let it be an extension of your body. Look after it and it will look after you,' he said and then he pulled out the beedi[32] resting above his ear and left the kitchen through the back door. There was still a while before the other chefs would come in and Khan Chacha had a whole lot of vegetables for me, which I cut and chopped earnestly.

'It's the weekend, double down on ...' Alice was shouting when she, Kathy and Chris walked in; they could not believe their eyes. Boxes full of chopped vegetables were neatly kept near the chef's stations. The routine of the day took over and when Nick politely requested that I peel the garlic, I offered to chop them instead. Nick was sweet, his resistance for me to chop was not out of insecurity but to protect me from another mishap. I assured him that I knew what I was doing.

For lunch, we ran at full capacity and had a waiting list for dinner. Having run my own café, I knew the food business could be tiring, but this stress was another level. A bunch of people who were serving hundreds barely got any time for themselves to eat or even to visit the toilet. We had our lunch breaks in rotation; no one got more than ten minutes

---

[32]Beedi: Tiny Indian cigar rolls

to finish their meal, and most of us ate at our stations. Alice, Kathy and some others just vacuum cleaned heaps of spaghetti Bolognese; Dino scarfed down two slices of mozzarella pizza; Chris, Nick, Mario, Ryan and Jason had some salad which Chris tossed up in bulk and crumbled it with soon-to-expire blue cheese and bacon. As for Gabby, I barely saw her eat; she had a cigarette and an espresso for breakfast, a parmigiano slice and a cracker for lunch and more coffee and cigarettes to fuel her day. I keenly but discreetly paid attention to what everyone was eating, hoping we would have a proper break, a sit-down lunch and someone would ask me to join them, but Friday had everyone by the storm. Khan Chacha was free from all the stress and panic flowing on the floor; he managed to take regular breaks for his namaaz and beedi, yet his station where the meat was chopped was never called out for delays; he always had what the chefs needed and if he was not around, Ajmal was well instructed to guide Jason to the odd rump or rib.

He came to me with his lunch box and asked me to join him outside. We pulled two plastic chairs and sat in the back alley; he opened his three-tiered steel tiffin; it was home food: a bunch of folded rotis[33], which had acquired the round shape of the container, stir fried potatoes and Dal-gosht[34]. He didn't bother to heat the food and was eating it at room temperature, which in London is colder than a refrigerator. He offered it to me but I declined politely.

'This life can wear you out quickly, don't get attracted by the vices people glorify as work. Get enough sleep, eat

---

[33]Rotis: Indian bread
[34]Dal Gosht: A subcontinental dish made with lentils and mutton

proper meals and get as much fresh air as you can,' he told me and then gestured to eat along. I obliged. He was a fast eater—in less than five minutes he had gone through his meal and ended it by sucking on the bone to get at the marrow. He then drank water from a worn-out plastic bottle, rinsed his mouth thoroughly before gulping it down. Even though he had been living in England for almost all of his life, his mannerisms were not anglicised like Arun's. He reminded me of my Baba and it occurred to me that I had forgotten to text him to check on his meal and medicines.

Around 4 p.m. there was a slight lull, similar to the one I used to experience at my café and then, as the sun descended, the pace in the kitchen picked up. It was 11 p.m. by the time we were done; Gabby did a briefing with the chefs, from which I and the cleaning staff were excluded. Once everyone left, Ajmal asked me to come near the refrigerator. Khan Chacha was there.

'When you run a large-scale kitchen, you have to have foresight and put processes in place, which save you time and reduce wastage. FIFO—First in, First out—this is the way to manage your inventory. The ingredients which are closest to expiry should be the first to be pulled out. As a chef, you won't be setting the refrigerator but you should make sure it's done in this manner. And keep an eye out for the expired stuff; you should not use that knowingly or by mistake,' he instructed and I listened without a word. To be honest, all I wanted to do was to go back to the hotel and sleep.

'Now get some rest, see you tomorrow at seven,' he said and left, putting Ajmal in-charge of locking the doors. I was walking back to the hotel, it was terribly cold but that was not the most uncomfortable part about being out at this hour;

there were these odd groups of men standing and smoking, the stench of garbage disposals took over the streets, which during the day smelt of flowers, coffee and baked goodies. On one blind turn, a muscular man dressed in a netted top, unbuttoned red overcoat, leather skirt, blonde wig and red lipstick emerged from the dark! He was trying to say something but before he could, I sprinted across the street with a dooming sense that he was following me. Those few yards seemed unending, and with each step, I felt someone would grab my shoulder. Upon reaching the hotel stairs, I looked back; there was no one.

I went to see Baba, he was asleep. Once inside my room, I switched on the kettle, took off my clothes, left them on the floor, added boiling hot water to a cup of instant noodles and went to the bathroom to take a hot shower. I sat in a bathrobe, scarfing through the noodles like the chefs did; a car went past on the street, lighting the room for a fleeting moment.

Sita

Over the next three weeks, I continued this rigour of starting my day at 7 a.m. and ending it around midnight. I was no alien to hard work but the mental pressure to perform in this kitchen was more gruelling than the hours itself. And if I ever thought of asking for a day off from the training, I would look at Khan Chacha; he was about sixty and he always managed to reach before I did. He lived in Southall, which when I checked it on the map, was a good half an hour away by tube. He had devoted himself to teaching me the basics of a restaurant. The mornings gave us a good few hours of dedicated practice before the others came in. Over the past few days, he taught me about how the brigade system works in a professional kitchen, where the executive chefs delegate most tasks while keeping the key ones to themselves. The training was not about how to cook food but more about how to adapt to the working style of a gourmet kitchen and master processes which allow you to manage volumes in a scarcely limited time, while retaining consistency. One morning, he just asked me to observe him carve out meat, saying, 'steaks and shanks are made on the butcher's table, not on the grill.'

'What happened?' he asked after I took a step back from the wooden slab where he was working.

'Nothing. It's just the beef … I don't eat it,' I confessed.

'It's all right, one should not be apologetic for what they believe in. I don't touch pork. For Arun it meant he had to hire another butcher and I respect him for that. There is always a way forward as long as we follow what we feel is right for us, but respect the feelings of others too,' he said.

Once I got to know Chacha more closely, I realised that beyond that intimidating persona, there was a humble and compassionate man. In the age of Spotify, he was a gramophone.

I learnt the nuances of a professional kitchen during the morning shifts and at night, he would leave, asking me to practice with the dishes which I believed in, which according to me would work at Bellissimo. Dishes which bore my own identity as a chef.

'You are not here to play a supporting role. In this kitchen you have to recreate that magic which Ben and Arun experienced in India. Find your own voice, your own food and then lead!' he had said, inspiring me to cook fearlessly. Since then, every night I experimented with dishes, recreating the ones I loved making at my café, often giving them a twist to suit the palate of Londoners.

'Never take your mise en place for granted, it's the key to—' he spoke while demonstrating the arrangement.

'What happened?' he paused and asked. The morning was particularly cold and for the first time, I felt a little irritable to have to go through the obvious things, perhaps for the third time since we began training.

'I know mise en place, I learnt it ...' I was talking and he interrupted me.

'Yes, you are not new to cooking and you obviously have some talent. That's why you are here, but in this kitchen, be like a white piece of paper,' he reprimanded and continued with the session.

Later, Ben came to see us. I had not seen him or Arun in over two weeks. He always wore bright colours: teal, fuchsia, turquoise, peach. A sharp contrast to the dark, dull and pastel colours Arun wore. He was talking to Khan Chacha and I was curious to see if he was taking a report on my progress, *'Have they decided to send me back? Did Khan Chacha call him to complain about the morning?'* These doubts were convoluting my mind when Ben approached me.

'Hey, how's it going?' he asked.

'Good. I've learnt a lot from Khan Chacha.'

'Yes, he told me. You learn fast.'

'How are things with you?' I asked.

'Been fine, work piles up in Arun's absence,' he said and read the curiosity on my face about Arun's whereabouts.

'He should be back tonight though,' he assured me and I did not bother asking further. Seeing us talk, Alice intervened; through my peripheral vision I could sense that she and Gabby were texting each other.

'Ben, my boy, we don't see much of you these days,' Alice said, patting Ben on the back.

'Hello, Alice, nice to see you. Work is keeping me busy,' he said rather formally. Ben was not fond of Alice either.

'And Arun? Where's he these days? At the perfumery?' she asked.

'No, he's away,'

'With that supermodel, what's her name? Zara ... Zerena, or a new one?' she smirked.

'I'm not sure,' he said in a reserved tone.

'Sita, have you soaked the morels I asked you to?' she turned to me and asked. She had never mentioned anything about the morels; it was a decoy.

'Yes, they're soaked,' I said, having coincidently soaked a batch for myself. 'You can use half. I'll use the rest for Aglio Olio,' the words slipped out of me, revealing what I was to do in the after-hours tonight.

'We're not serving Morel Aglio Olio,' Gabby came and overruled.

'They sound delicious, similar to what we ate in Himachal,' Ben intervened.

I sighed in relief, they thought I was talking about introducing a dish on the menu.

'This isn't Himachal. Anthony has truffle-infused Aglio Olio on his menu, we surely don't want to copy him.' she told Ben.

'And in this kitchen, I decide the menu. So, if you have

ideas—and it's good to have ideas, they can come from anyone—but first, you run them past me,' she said with a brooding sense of authority. I did not respond, unwilling to challenge her position but the animosity running as an undercurrent so far had suddenly transformed into a flash flood.

Later in the day, Khan Chacha and I sat down for lunch. It was too cold outside and of late we had been eating at the far end of the kitchen to get some respite from the madness.

'They're aware you're up to something. Have your menu ready and present it to Arun when he's back,' he said. 'How long has it been?' he then asked, referring to the time we had begun our training.

'Three weeks,' I said.

'Hmmm... there's still some way to go. Keep practicing and keep observing,' he encouraged me and then we started eating. Chacha was so considerate, he had doubled his tiffin quantity since I joined. He may have been used to eating his food cold but for me, he had started heating it in a microwave. Today he had brought Biryani, which honestly, was the best Biryani I had ever eaten.

'How's your Baba doing?'

'He's fine,' I said. I wish I could tell him the truth. It had been a week since I had last seen him awake. He would be asleep when I left and came back. Chacha figured that out from my response.

'Take some hours off today. Take him out for tea, come back by seven,' he insisted.

'But ...'

'Don't worry. I'll tell Gabby and Ajmal will cover for you,' he assured and I did not argue further. Without wasting much time, I rushed back to the hotel.

Baba was watching television in his room, at first, he ignored me. I tried to cajole him but he was upset, and rightfully so. I had taken him away from the vast sublimity of the mountains and locked him up in a room, so what if the room happened to be in London? In a desperate attempt to uplift his mood, I conveyed that we would get ice-cream; over the years, an ice-cream bribe never failed to soften him.

We stepped out, the icy winds were slapping us, walking was near impossible and we hopped on and off the red buses as much as we could to arrive at a Christmas market on the South Bank. It was not even 4 p.m. but it felt like 7 p.m.; the sky was ablaze with hues of violet, amber and maroon. We were under a canopy of lights as if all the stars in the universe had descended to celebrate Christmas. The children were lining up for the carousel and a group of musicians were playing the guitar, trombone, saxophone and the accordion. Narrow lanes with stalls of gifts and food on either side, stopped the cold breeze from the river from penetrating the market, people were frolicking about the place without any fear with only smiles to wear—it was a reassuring sight after all the world had been through.

Before we could settle on what to do, Baba had already spotted an ice-cream seller. He was looking at the myriad flavours, unable to decide which one he would pick, but finally landed on the mint chocolate chip for its invitingly green colour. I chose the strawberry cheesecake. The musicians on the rampart acknowledged us with a smile; their tune was infectious, it had my head shaking, my foot tapping and my hands clapping. Seeing me, Baba too started doing the same. He had never heard the sound of music or any sound for that matter, yet he was tuned in to the rhythm of life; seeing him let himself free, dancing like a little kid in the rain, filled my heart with joy. He was expressing his excitement as best as he could. His zeal was so contagious, the passers-by joined him in that out-of-sync but joyous dance. This impromptu and free-spirited performance earned a thunderous applause from the spectators and both Baba and I were numb from the experience. Seeing him so gleeful, I could redeem myself from the guilt of not having spent time with him.

We were walking along the narrow ramparts between the stalls; everything from a keychain to a hat was prohibitively expensive. I tried a muffler but it was twenty-five pounds; back in Shimla, I could get the exact same piece at one fifth of the price. From the souvenir shop, Baba picked up a glass sphere with a snowman inside; he shook it and it turned into a ball of glitter. He looked at it in amazement and then he saw the price—it was fifty pounds! He kept it back. I could not see his heart break like that and I purchased it. His joy was unbound. Then we ate some cheese balls with fondue and had hot mulled wine. Baba insisted on having another glass but I did not want him to lose his senses.

London glittered brighter in the Thames. Baba saw the London Eye up-close for the first time and started pulling at my sleeve. Realising it was a giant Ferris wheel—something he loved since his childhood during all the Dusshera[35] fares in our village—he insisted we go for a ride. I went to the ticketing counter but the queue for the Eye was too long and I had to be back at the restaurant. With much reluctance, Baba agreed to let the ride pass, but to keep his heart, I clicked a

---

[35]Dusshera: Hindu festival

selfie of the both of us with the Eye in the background. In my heart, I kept feeling guilty for this consolation prize. We went back to the hotel but this was not without a promise from me to take the ride on our next outing.

❧

Ben

'*To the Batcave, Alfred,*' I mimicked Arun in my head; amusing how he would say these words when he would see me at the arrival terminal. The family chauffeur and I were headed to pick him up in his black Jaguar. He had taken off for Gstaad with Zerena after his daughter had declined the trip.

'*With Zerena in his suite, he'd be zonked to do any skiing,*' I pictured while waiting. Dressed in a mahogany leather jacket with a beige fur lining and black jeans, he looked his dishiest best as he walked straight past me and placed his luggage in the boot. Zerena was not with him. He nodded slightly, which by now I knew meant: *I know you have been fine.*

'Zerena?' I asked.

'Don't bother,' he said and not to my surprise—things were over between them. Ever since his divorce, he had struggled to stay invested in one woman beyond a financial quarter.

'We have a two-year lock in on the Herne Hill apartment lease, Arun,' I reminded him of his hormonally-driven generosity.

'Figure it out,' he said, expecting me to solve this for him.

'*Waqar bhai, Ma ke ghar le chalo,*' he told his chauffeur, though I could not comprehend Hindi, I understood that we were going to his parent's house for their traditional Christmas dinner.

'How's it going?' he asked, referring to Sita's progress. During his trip, he would periodically check in with me, mostly to be reassured that Sita had not left. Arun and Sita had not spoken since his outburst. He had visited the restaurant a couple of times since the incident but kept to his office, avoiding a run in with her. He was not the kind of person who would walk up and apologise for his outburst and was hoping that time would thaw things organically. He was relieved to know that Khan Chacha had taken her under his wing. If there was one man apart from me who he trusted blindly, it was Khan Chacha.

We arrived at his parent's landed house in Kensington; it was even more grand than the house Arun had in Richmond. The floor was all marble, there were two large oil paintings on the walls of the passage leading to the living room—one of an Indian God with blue skin, playing the flute and the second was an impressionist version of Ganesha. Their living room was like a Sotheby's auction house with illustrations and paintings of varying sizes including two elusive pieces, one by the Indian artist Raza and the other was a landscape by Constable. A wall was designated for a brooding life-size portrait of Arun's grandfather, the placard read '*Dewan Bahadur Parmeshwar Mehra,*' the perfume and essential oil merchant who migrated to England in the years after India attained sovereignty. A two-tier crystal chandelier hung from the centre of the ceiling, illuminating the room in diffused tungsten light. Then there was an engraved ivory tusk placed on a wooden stand, and above it was a black and white photograph. Arun never failed to tell me the story involving his great-grandfather and Viceroy

Mountbatten, how they both took one tusk each of the beast they had slain during a hunting camp at the foothills of the Himalayas. The curtains and upholstery were of the most expensive brocade and velvet money could buy, and period statues and vases were scattered in different corners of the hall. His mother, Lata Mehra, welcomed us. Though she was in her mid-sixties, she was always full of beans. She was wearing a fine silk saree with a cashmere shawl.

She and the house butler led us to the dining room. Since I shadowed Arun during all his waking and non-copulating hours, I was also the unintentional guest to this dinner for the past three years. Natasha, Amira and his father, were already seated when we entered; Amira ran and hugged her father and then we took our seats.

Arun's father, Balraj Mehra, reminded me of my own grandmother. They both were pathologically infatuated with traditions that did not exist anywhere but in their own heads and they both had a partisan loyalty to the royals. For Arun's family, their imperial inclination was linked to their business ties to Buckingham, but my grand old lady had missed the Suez syndrome; from her window she could still see the fabled sun which never sets. On the table, Arun was facing his own Swiss syndrome. Up until yesterday, he was skiing through the plush peaks of the Alps with Zerena and now he was at a dining table with his mother, ex-wife, daughter and an austere father who perceived Arun's restaurant as a hobby rather than a real business.

Amira and Mrs Mehra were talking relentlessly and at one point it seemed difficult to tell who among the two was a child. Honestly, I looked forward to this dinner for my annual dose of family drama, having not had much to call a family for myself. The food was good but my intolerance for spice was never a consideration for Mrs Mehra and her cook. Arun's grandmother was wheeled in by her caregiver. An octogenarian, age had enfeebled some of her faculties but none of her grace. Arun, Natasha and Amira got up to touch her feet and she gave each of them a peck on their cheek. She inquired about how Natasha and Amira were.

'Are you sure you won't eat, Dadima?' Natasha asked.

'I am fine, beta. Age doesn't agree with supper anymore. But I have made apple pie for you,' she said and Amira's face lit up. She sought a reaction from Arun too but he was visibly preoccupied. Arun loved everything his grandmother baked and even though she baked less frequently now, whenever she did, he would come over to eat with her.

'Don't you worry my chaand[36], you'll earn your star again,' his grandmother said comfortingly. Back in Himachal, Arun callously remarked that he did not need an endorsement from a tyre company, but the loss of the elusive star was showing on his face and on the balance sheet. His grandmother knew his predicament and though her thoughts were well intentioned, the family dinner table was not the right place to bring it up.

'They gave the star to that Italian chef, Tony. It'll not come back. Restaurants have a short shelf life and if you are satisfied after this prolonged hobby of yours, it's not too late to take the reins of your real business,' his father jibed.

I could sense Arun's rage. He looked at his mother who was pleading with her son to not start an argument with her stubborn husband. Arun was already dealing with a lot to keep the restaurant and its reputation afloat and the last

---

[36]Chaand: My moon

thing he needed was a taunt from his father.

He got up from the table and stormed out.

Sita

It was well past eleven, everyone had left, I was experimenting with some dishes that were a blend of traditional Italian and Indian flavours and Ajmal was helping me with the preparations. We heard someone jostle with the back door. I had locked it from the inside, fearing Alice or Gabby would show up. I stopped the plating midway and asked Ajmal to check who was there. He peeped in through the square glass and had a panic-stricken expression on his face; he opened the door hastily.

It was Arun. He walked in, lurching through the narrow channels between the stations.

'What's this?' he asked, his voice slurred, reeking of cigarette and alcohol, a smell I was not unfamiliar with. Baba occasionally used to come back in a similar state.

'Nothing, I was just …' I was trying to explain when he took a spoon from the counter and dug into the Keema Lasagna lying in front of me. He ate a big bite. He was generally a sophisticated eater but today he was scarfing down the food like a truck driver stopping for dinner after a long drive; he ate a bit and then he ate some more.

'Are we serving this to customers?' he asked.

'No.'

'What the hell!' he said and gestured deliriously, conveying that he would be back in a moment and then he tiptoed to his office. I was nervous, certain that he would come back and fire me. Arun returned after five minutes. His face was washed, hair wet and neatly combed and he had fumigated himself with copious amounts of cologne to camouflage the alcohol.

'What do we have here, take me through it.'

'It's not ready yet ...' I said, but he overruled.

'It will never be ready—don't wait for the ducks to line up, show me what we have!' he asserted, instilling some confidence in me.

'Well, I was experimenting with Italian and Indian-fusion recipes,' I said and he signalled towards the dishes, asking to taste them and for me to explain what I had done.

'This is Keema Lasagna. I made it using keema masala instead of the traditional minced meat and used Kalari, the stringy Kashmiri cheese in place of mozzarella. And I also replaced ricotta with freshly made cottage cheese. But the Parmesan, it's still there,' I said. Arun ate some more of it. I probed for a response but he concealed his reaction.

'What else have we got?' he asked.

'This is Haak Ravioli,' I said, offering him some ravioli where I had replaced spinach with the Kashmiri green Haak.

'This needs more cheese, what else can you prepare?' he tasted one piece and said.

'Aubergine Cannelloni with the flavours of Baingan Bharta[37], Aalu Matar[38] Gnocchi and Himalayan Aglio Olio for the pasta. Then there is Nihari Ossobuco, Fritto Misto

---

[37]Baingan Bharta: An Indian dish made with aubergines
[38]Aalu Matar: A potato and peas dish

Pakoras[39] and Nadru Pizza,'

'Nadru as in lotus stem?'

'Yea, we call it Bhey in Himachal but on pizza, Nadru sounds better,'

'Hmm ... I want to try these things,' he said.

'All of them?'

'Yes!' he said firmly.

'I ... I don't have them ready ...' I said apologetically, I shouldn't have, he didn't ask me to make these things.

'Then make them,' he ordered and looked at Ajmal, who immediately launched into the preparations.

'Let me know when they are ready. I'm in my office,' he said and left. It was midnight and I had been cooking all day without letting the tiredness get to me. I turned on the tap, put my face under running water, went to the fridge, opened a can of cola, played some music and got down to business. Ajmal was surprisingly under-utilised; he had a sound knowledge of cooking and processes. We cooked for over two hours, preparing multiple dishes in tandem. Once the dishes were made, I paid attention to plating them.

I went to Arun's office and peeped in through the frosted glass door, which was transparent on the outside. He was lying on the sofa.

'Come in,' he said. Sensing I was there, he got up and opened his eyes wide to push the sleep away. I too had done this half a dozen times tonight. Though I had been working here for weeks, this was the first time I had seen his office—a wooden table and chair were at the far end, a sofa set was against the wall next to the door with a half-filled decanter

---

[39]Pakoras: Fried snacks with varied fillings

at the corner. There was a photo booth with a light box, presumably for food photography and there were multiple tennis racquets and horse racing photographs hanging from the walls.

'Is it ready?' he asked and I confirmed. He took his notebook and we left for the kitchen. He saw the dishes and sampled some, taking notes and cleansing the palate between each serving with a bottle of sparkling water. I could never get foreigners' fixation with sparkling water; back at my café we used to run out of them quickly during the tourist season and had to stock our pantry with multiple cartons. I would regularly ask Chotu's father to get these exorbitantly priced fancy sodas in bulk.

'You've plated them rather conservatively,' he commented.

'Exactly, the food is fusion. I didn't want to throw the customers off with too much of a surprise.'

'Patrons, not customers,' he said and then he tried more food, starting with the Nihari Ossobuco, where I chose the classic Italian Ossobuco but made it with a slow-cooked lamb shank in mild spices from the legendary Indian meat dish Nihari. I paired it with Nizami Risotto, which was basically risotto made with saffron infusion and garnish.

'The lamb needs to be more tender,' he said.

'Yes, it needs to be cooked for at least four hours. I didn't have that time right now,' I defended. He went on to try the Aubergine Cannelloni and a couple of other dishes and then I offered him a slice of pizza.

'Let the pizza be,' he said.

'But you haven't even tried it ...' I urged.

'We don't fuck with pizza, it's sacrosanct,' he asserted and though I felt it was quite condescending of him to disregard the pizza without trying it, I did not see a point in arguing.

'Do we have ingredients to make more of these?' he asked and Ajmal confirmed it.

'Great, have seven samples of each ready by 8 a.m.,' he ordered, waited for a moment to see if I would object and then left for his office. I was standing there, unable to frame my thoughts. It was the white-noise of emotions. My heels were aching, my eyes refusing to stay open and my head felt like someone was playing tabla inside. *'This is your chance to redeem yourself, claim it!'* I told myself and buried the urge to rest or quit.

7

Happy New Year

Ben

$\mathcal{J}$ was in the kitchen with my to-go latté. Arun had sent us a message in the middle of the night, calling us to the restaurant at 8 a.m., Khan Chacha, Mario, Jason, Ryan, Gabby, Philip and I were the tasting jury. I was the only non-chef in this ensemble. Philip too had trained as a chef but his managerial skills led him to become a veteran of the front operations.

Arun had this litmus test for all new dishes introduced at the restaurant. The tasters tried them blindfolded. According to him, it allowed an uncontaminated critique of the taste, which was not biased by how the dish appeared. One station was cleared for the tasting. We all had put on our eye masks. I could hear a member of the serving staff place the plates in front of us. He then handed us teaspoons while Arun narrated the instructions.

'Last night I tried a few dishes and I want you all to tell me how you feel about them,' he asked us. He had probably made up his mind about what he had tasted and what he would do with it, but he was seeking consensus—not so much from a place of self-doubt but a 'told you so' to his narcissistic self. In my first such tasting, I prompted a response immediately after eating the dish and Arun was swift to reprimand me. After everyone had sampled what was served, the server would then remove the plates and the tasters would take off their eye masks and make notes on what they ate, so one's opinion did not influence another's.

We sampled the first dish. The spice was unbearable but thank god there was a glass of water for palate cleansing. I downed all of it the moment I was able to take my mask off. This exercise of blindfolding, tasting and jotting our feedback was followed for six more dishes, with each dish tasting different from the other. I was puzzled by this assortment. The texture was surely Italian but the flavours were like curry. Sita stood in a corner like a zombie on double shift but her anxiousness seemed to be keeping her awake. After we finished eating, it was time to discuss our feedback.

'Gabby?' asked Arun.

'It's Indian food!' she freaked. Philip, Jason, Mario and Ryan also pointed out that they thought they were sampling Indian food. Their comments though were minus the derogation Gabby laced her's with. Then Arun asked for my opinion.

'The fusion is unique but a little on the hot side!' I remarked.

'Valuable input. That's a big fraction of our patrons, Sita. Let's cut down the heat,' Arun told Sita and she nodded.

'And, don't over egg the pudding, infuse the Indian flavours but in pinches, not with a free hand,' he said.

'Pudding? I didn't make any,' Sita whispered to me.

'It's a phrase, silly! I'll tell you,' I hushed. She needed a little more of the London air to grasp that British vocabulary.

'Khan Chacha?' Arun asked; the old man had a smile of fulfilment on his face.

'Masha Allah! Nihari fusion with the Lombard Ossobuco on a bed of Zafrani[40] Risotto,' he lauded with a faint sense of nostalgia, like how one feels on finding an old photograph while cleaning the house.

'You aren't seriously thinking of rolling this out?' Gabby asked incredulously.

'That's exactly what I am thinking, GR!' Arun referred to Gabby by her initials. Gabriel Rossetti, or Gabby as we all called her, had joined Bellissimo four years ago. Arun and Anthony spotted her on Instagram while she was travelling through the Italian countryside, exploring provincial cuisines. Soon they both were on a plane to Rome to offer her a package astonishing for a sous chef. Her originality started defining the Sunday brunch at Bellissimo, and on other days, she freed up Anthony from the micro-managerial chores so he could really focus on his artistry and bag that famed star. In the process, she too grew into the mould of an ace sous chef who was touted as the next big thing on the British and European food scene.

'Arun, people come to us for authentic Italian food. This will damage us,' Gabby refuted with a sense of defensiveness, like a goalkeeper facing a penalty shootout.

'I concur. These flavours will surprise our guests and it may not be a pleasant one,' remarked Philip, his voice echoing

---

[40]Zafrani: Saffron infused

through the kitchen. There was silence, what they said made sense. Bellissimo had worked hard to carve a niche as an Italian gourmet destination and to suddenly pivot to something like this could be suicidal. Arun opened his tablet and started browsing through some screenshots he had taken.

'When Anthony left us in April, our rating was 4.8. By August, 4.4, and today 4.1. You can type 3.9 on my tombstone!' he screeched. 'It's nothing to take away from you Gabby, it isn't—you've been fantastic. Everyone in this kitchen tips their hat to you for keeping us afloat when we were left in the eye of the storm. But the truth is that Anthony was great, he was great when we started and then he grew complacent. We should be thankful that his exit gave us a chance to reinvent. The stillness of comfort is where excellence succumbs and mediocrity thrives and we are not fucking mediocre!' he exclaimed and the last phrase was a war cry.

'Repeat after me—WE ARE NOT FUCKING MEDIOCRE!' he yelled and our chorus followed, once, twice and thrice. Some voices were loud and in unison, but some remained mere lip-syncs. We all had to act out of genuine inspiration or obligation, the man still wrote everyone's paycheck.

'And remember—say this to yourself, not out loud but in your head so the words oscillate in your heart and soul—I will never be afraid to make mistakes,' he reinforced in his staff a sense of self belief and ability to be fearless, which through the years, had given us an edge over the other restaurants.

'But I take your point, this can throw our patrons off,' Arun acknowledged and then he created a little contest of sorts, something he loved doing to his employees by passing on his competitive spirit to them.

'On the first of February, we will test two set menus, one: the peasant cuisine, Cucina Povera, representing the finest and the most elemental of Italian food, its soul. This will be curated by Gabby, Mario, Dino and Alice,' he said.

'The other will be an Italian-Indian fusion menu, a confluence of not only flavours but of two cultures—Sita and Khan Chacha will spearhead this experiment,' Arun announced and took a pause, nibbling on some chopped dry fruits kept in front of him.

'We'll have an elaborate tasting event to judge which one of these menus will headline our relaunch this spring,' he concluded. There were mixed reactions among us but no one was bold enough to voice them. His speech had been inspirational but the idea of serving Indo-Italian fusion felt like asking the late Pavarotti to sing ghazals. Arun's father was big on the latter, any afternoon when I would land at his place, the gramophone would be playing a Jagjit Singh number. At first it felt odd, but after frequent trips the music grew on me as well, no different than how one takes to corduroys as a fabric.

'You have a full month to prepare. And Philip, look at the books—anything that hasn't been ordered at least once a week for the past six months, goes off the menu,' he said and Philip nodded.

'One last thing, Sita! From tomorrow you start as a station chef. Gabby, Alice has a lot on her plate—divide the load,' he ordered. Sita looked at me and I gave her a short smile, she deserved this right from the start.

Everyone dispersed to resume operations for the day, but Gabby and Sita stood there, absorbing what lay in front of them. Gabby particularly knew what was on offer—a chance to become one of the foremost culinary exponents on the London food scene but Sita, I doubt she could fathom the magnitude of opportunity she had just been presented with. The thing with opportunities is, for most people they come in disguise, so it is not until years later that one can look back and assess those whispering instances in life to realise if one took or missed their chance. But for Sita, it wasn't fate whispering in her vicinity but destiny thudding on her door. The question for her and everyone was—can she seize the moment?

Sita

All of London was in a festive spirit, but for us at Bellissimo, the workload had double-decked, much like the city buses. The distinction between weekdays and weekends had blurred. Today, we all reported early and Gabby was holding a meeting for the entire staff.

'Tonight is a goldmine—good food and service will get us great reviews but bad food and service will bury us,' she said, making eye contact with me.

'I want you all to give your absolute best—forget it's the New Year's Eve—not for us. For us, it's the most important working night of the year. We'll be open till 1 a.m. Philip, is the permit in place?'

'Yes, Chef,' confirmed Philip.

'Good! Recommend our finest wines to the couples, they'll be willing to splash tonight,' she added.

'And Sita, you have a big responsibility. Keep the pastas

on simmer and prepare them al dente as the orders come,' she said. I affirmed. In my new role as the chef de partie or station chef, I was to manage everything to do with pasta. My chef's coat was still not here though. After that disastrous first day in the kitchen, I think Ben was reluctant to order a new coat for me. I was working in an apron like the commies.

'And don't fuck it up!' she said sternly, adding more weight to the mental pressure I had piled over myself.

I was nervous about growing into this responsibility but was equally excited to find a prominent place for myself. It was my chance to regain lost pride and prove myself worthy. The debriefing continued till the service hours began. The lunch went off smoothly but come 6 p.m. we all were like fish caught in a strong current, overwhelmed by the bookings and the high stakes for the night. People were ordering the most expensive and expansive food from the menu.

'Hotpot!' Ryan yelled, keeping a giant pot on the slab for cooling. Dino had prepared a dozen chocolate rum cakes and within the first couple of hours, they were all sold out. Jason was sweating profusely in front of the flaming grill; everyone wanted the finest cuts of steak for their last dinner of the year. Philip had to hire an extra barman to cater to the guests and most tables were done with their first bottle of wine and were ordering the next. While everyone was in sheer panic, it was only Khan Chacha and Gabby who were able to keep this tent pegged to the ground.

'It's a riot outside, most places turn into a disco bar with bank-breaking cover charges,' Ryan said, standing next to me with three live saucepans—each with a different sauce.

'We'll also have dance?' I asked.

'God forbid, no! We have a reputation to maintain. Today

there are no walk-ins. We only take advance reservations and screen the civil folks from the plebs,' he commented and then got busy with his work, leaving the conversation abruptly.

'Congratulations,' Kathy whispered. We now had stations facing each other.

'I tried some of your Haak Ravioli; it's really good,' she complimented but I was barely able to hear her amid all the shouting. Her red hair, noticeably skinny frame and pale skin were the first things one would notice about her, but I remembered her as one of the few who were genuinely concerned when I had cut my finger. In the past few days, I also realised she was extremely diligent with her work.

'Thanks,' I reciprocated.

'I heard about the tasting challenge. Best of luck. Let me know if you ...' she was saying in a muted tone.

'Just do your goddamn work!' Alice barged in and screamed. 'Is this a fucking picnic in a park?' she yelled.

Kathy was around ten years older than Alice but it did not stop Alice from humiliating her in front of everyone. The pace in the kitchen was so intense that no one stopped to notice this. Kathy was in tears but still carried on with her work.

'Rigatoni alla Carbonara! Service for table seven. Malloreddus with clams. Service for table twenty! Move aside. Hurry the fuck up! Jason, Ribeye medium-rare, Arista with plum wine sauce.' Random words flew through the air like arrows. In a span of a few hours, we all had exhausted the kitchen inventory along with our physical ability, all in the service of our customers. There was just a thin wall separating the mayhem in the kitchen from the symphonic calm of the dining room.

At five minutes to midnight, we all stopped working and

went out. The restaurant was lit with candles and a pianist was playing near the fireplace. There were some families in the dining hall: one with three kids, aged two to fourteen, and there were a few elderly people who had come in groups or as couples. They all were well dressed and gracious. I guess they had to be, if they could afford to eat here. From the glass door and the large windows opening into the street, I saw people in large numbers, running and yelling; it didn't look like they were celebrating.

'Ten, nine, eight … three, two, one,' Philip was counting down in his deep baritone, four crew members popped open the champagne bottles to bring in the new year. The bubbly was first served to the guests and later, the staff had it in the kitchen, mostly from the bottle, while it changed multiple hands and mouths, forgetting what havoc such a behaviour had wreaked upon the world in the first place. Everyone greeted and hugged each other and five minutes later—we were back to serving the final orders for the night.

Arun and Ben came in through the back door, they brought a giant cake and two bags full of what looked like gifts; we had just called it a night.

'It's our annual tradition. Arun brings in gifts for everyone and all the sales on New Year's Eve are equally distributed among the staff as a token of appreciation,' said Ryan.

'Good way to ring in the new year,' added Jason. Even though everyone was celebrating, Kathy particularly was not over the yelling; she seemed frightened since then.

'Happy New Year,' Arun came and wished reservedly.

'Happy New Year,' I responded with a gentle smile.

'How are you doing?' he asked.

'I am good, and you?'

'Been fine,' he quipped and then paused. He seemed a bit odd; it felt like he wanted to say something more but he did not.

'How's the preparation coming along?' he inquired.

'Good.'

'Let's have the cake!' he offered.

'Sure,' I agreed and we joined everyone for the celebrations. This man continued to perplex me. For the most part, he had a straight face and was cunningly focused on his work, much like all businessmen are, irrespective of which part of the world they operate in or what the scale of their business is. Then he was unapologetically self-centred and that impulsive rage was a different matter altogether, but he also was infectiously inspiring and these odd instances of generosity did not add up to the larger image one would paint of him. I guess that's why people worked for him, you need to balance your vices with your virtues to find a place in this society.

We were winding up operations for the night. Alice, Gabby and Dino did not have any qualms about discussing their celebration plans out loud. They asked Arun to join them and when he declined their offer, they left. We worked at the same restaurant, some of us did the same jobs and broadly were in the same age brackets, but they felt like they belonged to this elite and entitled club of individuals where admission was by birth, not different from the archaic caste system my people still followed back home. After they had left, everyone else started to disperse as well.

'Ben will drop you,' Arun offered.

'I'm fine. I usually go back alone,' I said, declining his generosity.

Later, I saw Kathy walking by herself in the back alley.

There were still some people in the streets, drunk enough to think they have the license to hug anyone and wish them a happy new year. It was bitingly cold and she shivered while walking to the bus stand.

'Hey! Happy New Year,' I wished.

'Thanks. Happy New Year to you too!' she said. She was kind but gullible and I guess all that bullying had a constant impact on her behaviour. She reminded me of how I was when I was alone, facing my fears and uncertainties.

We walked over to the bus stop. She looked at her phone to check the time and I could not help but notice her wallpaper, an image of her holding a boy of about eight or nine.

'It's okay, you can leave. The next bus is in half an hour,' she said, aware that I was peeping at her phone screen.

'No, I can stay ...'

'It's fine, Sita, I am fine. Happy New Year,' she insisted. What we see of other people is only the surface and with each layer, our perception of who they are changes. In this brief interaction, I could only make assumptions and connect the dots about what her life would be like.

Ben

We had just finished a stack of eggy bread with strawberries, the short-lived and rare winter sun was filtering in through the bedroom while I lay in slumber with my head in Mark's lap; if tranquillity could ever be captured in a moment, this would be it.

'Hey, check this out,' Mark said, bringing his phone in front of my face. 'Let's drive to Wycombe and spend the weekend at this Airbnb,' he proposed, caressing my hair.

'One—it's not Wycombe anymore, two—look at the snow, it's brass monkeys outside and three—It's just Friday, I can't take the day off.'

'Let's see about that,' he teased, trailing his hands down my collar and intensifying the massage in my head.

'Are you sure you won't take off …' he whispered, circling his thumb around my nipples while his lips trailed around my neck. His breath gave me goosebumps.

'All right, all right … stop it!' I resisted. 'I'll take an off, let me ask Arun.'

Mark's expression changed; he was not fond of Arun—perhaps jealous that my boss got to see so much more of me. I was in a dilemma about what to tell Arun, lying did not come naturally to me but I also aspired to a life where watching sunsets was a routine and not a luxury. I texted Arun, asking if I could take the day off without giving an explanation. While waiting for a response, I saw Mark standing in the distance at the kitchen counter, brewing tea in his chequered boxers. His back muscles flexed as he moved his hands and that mocha skin shone under the shaft of light coming in from the kitchen window. Arun responded with a 'Sure…' and that was it! I had been dreading having to find an excuse and he did not even bother to seek one.

I went up to the kitchen and hugged Mark from behind, nibbling at his earlobe. 'Pack the bags, we're going!' I said and we kissed passionately. My phone started buzzing. I let it be, nothing was more important at that moment. Once the boiling kettle sought Mark's attention, I returned to the bed and the phone buzzed again—it was Sita. Had it been anyone else, I would have declined the call.

'Ben!' she yelled from the other side.

'Hello, Sita, is everything fine?' I asked, sensing panic in her tone.

'No, Ben! The hotel is saying we can't stay anymore,' she replied frantically.

'Gosh!' I just remembered her stay was only for a month. *'It's just a month since we came from India? it feels like forever.'* I wondered.

'Let me talk to the hotel manager,' I asked and she passed on the phone.

'Hi, good morning. I want to check if we can extend their stay by a week?'

'Good morning, Sir. My apologies, that will not be possible, we are completely sold out. I had even left two reminders for the guests,' came the manager's apologetic but clipped reply.

'Anything else I can help you with today?' he pressed and I responded with a helpless thank you.

'Don't worry, ask for a late checkout. I'll figure this out,' I told Sita. Mark was here with our tea; it did not take much for him to guess that our plan was no longer possible. I tried to offer an explanation but none could work; he put on his blue jeans, brown sweater and black varsity jacket, and stormed out. I felt a twinge of guilt about not worrying about him at that moment but the urgency to find a shelter for Sita overshadowed that guilt. I checked other hotels online, all of London was sold out—people ended up travelling an awful lot more after they could, the only booking I found was for an economy bed and breakfast on the outskirts of the city. I certainly could not lodge Sita there. Arun would have me for dinner.

'*Zerena is still at Herne Hill!*'

It suddenly occurred to me and I swiftly booked an Uber. Last week, I had dropped her a text asking her to transfer the lease in her name or evacuate.

It was not until the fourth bell that someone answered to let me up the stairs. A lanky man in glittering pyjamas and unbuttoned shirt opened the door; the house was in shambles, clouded with smoke and blaring with noise some people misinterpreted as music. Strangers were scattered across the living room, smoking cigarettes, joints and bongs. Paper glasses and half-eaten pizzas were littered about the floor. I found the switchboard and pulled out the plug, the Alsatian-sized speaker went mute and the chihuahua-size phone continued to play.

'Oh, Ben. Welcome darling. Happy New Year,' Zerena breathed. I wished cordially.

'Join us for prana meditation?' she asked. She was dressed in loose psychedelic pyjamas and shirt, like the hippies of the sixties had been resurrected. Last I saw of her, she had the sheen of a gazelle, but now I wondered if she had acquired this phoney gypsy avatar after Arun broke up with her—or did he finally have a revelation that beyond those plush lips and biscuity body, there was a squirrel sized brain?

'I'd love to, sweetheart, but I have business to attend to. Meanwhile, the rent is due this week,' I said, handing her a receipt.

'But I thought …', her breeziness had breezed past her, she was trying to find an argument but I made it quick for both of us.

'It's okay darling. You can pay the dues and stay, or Arun would pay for the last month and you can pack and leave today. I see you have a lot of people who can help you with that.'

'What's the matter?' a random bloke inquired.

'Keep out of this,' I asserted.

'But Ben, where will I go honey?' she began to soften up, knowing I meant business.

'I'm sure your friends have space for you, and if not, we want to do this the right way—there is an Airbnb a little far out from here. I can book you there for a week,' I offered. She was rendered speechless. I would have been a little gentler with all this had she not been an opportunist who had cancelled the lease on her old apartment within a week of realising that her new lover was giving her an upgraded life.

'I'm taking the keys so you don't have to bother with returning,' I said, picking up the house keys from the hook. 'And sweetheart, the deep cleaning services are scheduled for 5 p.m. today.' I gave her the ultimatum and left. Was it right, what I did? Perhaps no, but do I regret it? Definitely not.

Sita

The apartment was well ventilated but it smelled of chemicals, camouflaged by synthetic air freshener. I had finished the work at the restaurant and it was almost midnight when Ben escorted us here. The house was manicured like a hotel, but it would take a few days of living here for it to feel like home. Baba was delighted to see this new place; it was the first time in his life that he had a new house to live in, in fact, it was the first time in a long time that he had had something new at all.

'One tube change and thirty minutes, that's all it'll take,' Ben explained. He had been extremely supportive, but at this point I just wanted him to leave so I could go to sleep. The hotel was far more luxurious but it allowed the worst sleep possible. Hopefully this would feel like my own bed. After he left, I did not even bother to unpack our suitcases; Baba was enthusiastically exploring every nook and corner of the house, switching every switch on and off, but I went straight to the master bedroom. The mattress did not have a sheet and I still had my apron tied halfway around my waist, without bothering to fix either, I lay down—my feet still on the floor, knees bent at the edge of the bed and back buried in the mattress. The next thing I knew, sunlight was illuminating the room.

The morning came with a challenge and a deadline. We were just three weeks away from the tasting contest. Khan Chacha and I had carried on with our routine of starting early in the kitchen to experiment with the dishes we would present for the competition. We were not alone though. Gabby, Mario, Alice and Dino had also started coming in early to detail out the agrarian cuisine they were to compete with.

'Focus here,' Khan Chacha scolded when I was distracted by some loud joke Alice had cracked.

'Remember, Sita, excellence is not about being basic at great things, it's about being great at things which are basic. Master your craft to the extent that it becomes an instinct,' he said. Chacha had this great habit of starting the day with some words of wisdom, something to inspire before getting down to the details.

'Now, our set menu comprises of seven courses. Course

one would be the Aperitivo, a bread basket and a spirit, which Arun curates himself. This will be decided after he knows what the entire food experience is like. For the second course—the Antipasti, or simply put, the starters—what do we have?' he asked.

'A charcuterie board?' I proposed.

'Be specific. Not just any cheese board, what are you putting on it?' he probed.

I was thinking spontaneously: our cue was Italian and Indian fusion, 'Ricotta and Gorgonzola from Italy,' I proposed.

'Why do you pick these two?'

'One is soft and sweet, the other firm and sharp. Nice contrasts.'

'Fair, but we need more.'

'Add to that lightly-seared Paneer with hing and ajwaian[41] powder, like a tikka. So the crust is golden brown, but the centre, still soft and moist. We can also add Bandel to the mix, provided we get it here,' I explained; the Bengali-Portuguese cheese was hard to find in India, forget England.

'Everything worth finding can be found in London,' he affirmed with great confidence.

'And along with olives, we can add some Indian gooseberries!' I said as the idea popped into my head.

'Now we are thinking fusion,' he spoke triumphantly. Khan Chacha's innate curiosity and his years at The Claridge's had given him expertise on the nuances of Italian gourmet food.

'For the meat, seek Mario's help. I don't work with pork but he knows his cold cuts well,' he added.

'Chacha, I was also thinking that for the antipasti, we can

---

[41]Hing and Ajwaian: Asafoetida and carom seeds

have Fritto Misto Pakoras—an assortment of batter-fried Indian pakoras made bite-sized and seasoned with Mediterranean herbs. It's naturally vegan but with some sardines we can have a pescatarian version. Here, I've made a batch,' I suggested, offering something which I felt was simple yet unique. Chacha sampled some of the onion and cauliflower pakoras.

'Mind you, it's a bold fusion. A blended take on household snacks from both these regions. The course will set the tone for the meal,' he said animatedly while nibbling on the fried gram flour fritters.

'Course three—Primi or the first main course—for this you must have a soup. We still need to work on something better,' he said and just when I was about to come up with a suggestion, he snapped, half-laughing. 'Don't mention the tomato soup!'

I had already been thinking of the soup options we could offer and the biggest challenge was to find something uniquely Italian and then to give it an Indian twist.

'Kulith Minestrone!' I prompted; a flash of innovation struck me. Taking the staple lentil from my region and marrying it with Italy's most popular soup would be interesting, but so far, I had only made it in my head. I was yet to experiment with it. *'How do I blend these two distinct flavours? At what stage and to what degree do I distort the original recipe while it retains its soul?'*

'Sounds promising. Make it and we shall see,' Khan Chacha stated. At the far end of the kitchen, Gabby and her team were in full swing, preparing their dishes and chirping constantly. I was not sure what they were making and it did not bother me as long as I was happy with what I was doing.

'For Primi, we also need a solid offering, something more

satiating than the first two courses, but still light enough to not fill you,' he said.

'What's on the shortlist?' he paused and asked.

'How about Keema Lasagna?'

'It'll be too heavy; avoid meat here,'

'Haak Ravioli?' I proposed and he smiled. Chacha had a knack for being a great sounding board for recipes which did not work. He would dive into your intuition, dish out the flaws you were trying to push under the carpet and he would articulate those problems out loud. And for the dishes that were promising, he would know them in an instant, like the Haak Ravioli in this case.

'That tastes good!' Alice commented, infiltrating our work station and picking a piece of the ravioli. Thankfully, I did not have to involve myself—one look from Chacha had her on the run like a buffalo upon seeing a tiger. Watching her flee, I enjoyed the moment like how the Hindi dubbed commentary plays on a wildlife television channel.

Every morning, from 9 a.m. to 11 a.m., we would do our preparations and then devote the day to the usual business. Thankfully, I was now able to come home a little early, which in the restaurant business still meant midnight.

When I reached home, Baba was elated to see me. He had unpacked and placed all our luggage in his room and mine. I felt guilty about putting him through all this at this age; barring a few hushed minutes in the morning, we barely got a chance to spend time together. He had finished his dinner but served some for me. I held his hands and assured him that I had eaten at work but he insisted I eat before I slept.

At the table he asked when I would take him to the Ferris wheel; I explained that the work was taking its toll on me but promised that we would go soon.

That night, I lay in bed, imagining how it would feel to win the tasting challenge, to have food curated by me being rolled out in England, to have my name on a menu like the names I saw on the flight menu. Just a few days ago, I did not even have a passport and here I was, in an apartment in London, competing for my dreams and destiny.

'Course four—the Secondi, the second main course and the highlight of an Italian meal—a make or break experience,' Khan Chacha said. Last night it had snowed heavily, and most people were late, allowing us to stretch our preparations by an hour.

'Can we have two options?' I asked.

'You can have three if you like and let the customers choose.'

'Nihari Ossobuco on a bed of Saffron Risotto, Himalayan Aglio Olio for vegans and Seared Salmon Malabari for pescatarians.'

'Perfect,' said Khan Chacha. He was irrevocably in love with the Nihari, ever since the first time he had it, he had asked me to make it twice more—once he even packed it for his wife and children.

'Lock these three. For course number five—we skip the Controni, which is a side accompanying the main—and move to Insalata, the salad,' he explained.

'I thought salad was served before the main course.'

'The Americans! Forget that,' he said dismissively.

'Caesar?' I proposed.

'Don't say that word again. Caesar belongs in the history books, not in a salad bowl. Those damn Americans!' he vented.

'By now, your experiments would have toe the line at

delivering fusion food, so bring the experience back to remind the guests that this is still Italian food. Keep it simple and keep it Italian,' he guided. I was caught in the whirlwinds of un-imagination regarding what would that be, nothing that I had on my list fit the mould.

'Mozzarella alla Caprese?' Khan Chacha suggested. 'Just replace the Mozzarella with seared Kashmiri Kalari and call it Cashmere—these goras know that word well. For them, every sheep is a roll of Cashmere,' he remarked.

'Cashmere alla Caprese! Sounds good and super simple to make,' I gave him a high five. He hesitantly clapped his hand against mine; in an unspoken but clear way, we both realised how much we were enjoying this process. For me, this was all I ever wanted to do and I was doing it at a place and at a scale I could not have fathomed in my dreams. For Chacha, he had been in the kitchen far too long as a butcher, doing what he is the best at while also absorbing and learning the whole process beyond his own domain—this was his chance to share it with me and with all of London.

'Course six—Dolce, the dessert!'

'Shikanji[42] sorbet,' I prompted, having been an ardent fan of chuski[43] in my village.

'Brilliant! The word sorbet comes from the Persian word—sherbet,' he said; the man was a compendium of food trivia. During our training, I learnt that Spaghetti with Meatballs was perceived as an offence in Italy and the dish was invented in the USA. Caesar salad too, had its origin in Mexico and had little to do with Italy. He also helped me understand the

---

[42]Shikanji: Masala flavoured lemonade
[43]Chuski: Ice lollies

subsects of Italian cuisine: how Roman, Sardinian, Lombard, Tuscan and Neapolitan cuisines were different from each other and the world at large used a third grade Xerox of Neapolitan food in the name of all things Italian.

'Old Monk Tiramisu—add that as a dolce option,' he suggested.

'You won't believe that's what I had at my café in Himachal!' I said animatedly.

'I'm sure that was great but to make a dessert at a fine dining restaurant, it has to be done by the pastry chef and for this, we will need his help,' he added, pointing towards Dino, implying that I go and seek his aid. I was unsure of his suggestion. Dino was the pastry chef but he was also in Gabby's camp. Chacha saw through my hesitation.

'Don't worry, he is a professional. He'll do it,' Khan Chacha affirmed. 'And remember, in life, it's better to ask for favours than settle for a consolation prize,' he said encouragingly and we both smiled.

'And the last course, Caffé ...' I interrupted him. This one I had thought about for too long.

'Filter Coffee Macchiato with Parle G! This was also a pairing I served at my own café and was a hit with the European backpackers,' I burst out with excitement and Khan Chacha agreed. We now had our set menu locked and what was left was for me to master its execution.

Kathy, Ajmal and I spent the next few days honing these dishes. In both of them I found the dream team to collaborate with.

'Is mint eaten a lot in India?' Kathy asked

'Yeah, it's a popular garnish and is used to make chutneys.'

'Should we use some on the Cashmere Salad?' She

suggested. I bought the idea instantly. Chacha had instructed me to master each dish on the menu but to dedicate attention to the Primi and Secondi, those two would be difficult to delegate even when cooked on a commercial scale.

Sprinting towards the contest, the days went like weeks but the weeks went like days and before I knew it, we were just one day away from the tasting event.

After a month of experimentation, we managed to put together a menu which blended these two stark palates. Today we had prepared the entire course for a dry run.

'How many people will come and taste this?' I asked.

'It depends on Arun. For a single new dish, he brings in ten people. So, for a set course, which will be the highlight of our relaunch, it could be all of Westminster,' Khan Chacha said.

That evening, Chacha left early, putting Mario in-charge of all the butchering. All through our preparations, he had been working like a twenty-something man but that sixty-something body had to give in; his knees were in excruciating pain. Not once did he complain while putting this menu together.

In the evening, I approached Dino.

'Hey.'

'Hello Sita.'

'If you don't mind, I need a favour,' I requested.

'Sure, how can I help you?' he asked politely but with a thick Italian accent, which was not all that bad—I was tired of the British elasticizing syllables with their 'h's and 'r's.

'Actually, for the testing menu I needed a version of Tiramisu …' I began to propose when Gabby came in.

'Sure, he'll make it for you, anything else you need?' she said and Dino agreed willingly.

'Sita, I want you to feel welcome here. Whatever

happened, happened in the past. You have earned your place in this kitchen,' she said, extending a handshake. I did not know whether to take her words at face value or keep my guard up.

'If you are done, you too take some time off,' she offered. I was unsure at first but then I agreed. Later that night, I was walking to the tube station when Alice, Gabby and a couple of their friends who were not from the restaurant ran into me.

'Sita!' yelled Alice, not in control of herself.

'How long since you've been here?' she asked.

'Two months.'

'Wow, feels like forever ...' she jibed with sarcasm.

'It's not too late for some good old ice-breaking. Come, it's ladies night at most places in Soho; we're on a bender,' she mentioned, putting her arm around my waist.

'Thank you, but I have to ...'

'Oh, come on!' she insisted, pulling me along.

'One drink,' Gabby asked politely, relieving me from Alice's clutch. I agreed reluctantly. We went to this tiny bar brimming with people and music where the drinks were flowing freely. Alice and the other girls ordered gin and tonic, Gabby ordered a scotch and I chose a margarita. From where I came from, such places were aspirational and such drinks, forbidden. I was no drinker, barring that one off escapade with my friends from school where we tried beer for curiosity; it tasted like someone had bottled it at a roadside men's urinal, which in India could be smelled from meters away. Other than that incident, my contact with alcohol was limited to throwing an empty bottle into the bin if Baba came back with one. I was tempted to try a margarita, it was an itch induced by the internet, not knowing how it would taste or what exactly goes into it. I did think of ordering an orange juice or a cola but talked myself out of such a decision, fearing the leg-pulling I would receive in this company. The other two girls were flatmates of Alice—one an aspiring theatre actor and the other, a Pilates instructor.

'You're not used to margaritas,' Gabby said, judging by my expression. I conceded.

'Kitchen gets hotter than the oven. I'm sure you know by now,' she said, taking a sip from her whisky.

'It does, but I love it,' I said.

'Don't we all,' she said with a straight face. We engaged in casual chatter—she asked about my background, where I had studied and who was at home. I was forthcoming and candid with her. Though we had our differences, I had admired her from the moment I saw her run the kitchen. Before I knew it, one drink became three.

The other girls were flirting with strangers.

'So, Sita! Do you have a boyfriend!' Alice came yelling and I shook my head in a reserved manner.

'What! I am sure you are getting some?' she slurred. I avoided answering.

'Noooo! Tell me you've had it before!' she whispered in astonishment.

'Come, let's get you some man meat for *suppahh*,' she announced with an unusual sound to the word. She then held me by my arm and headed to the dance floor.

'Let it be,' Gabby came to my rescue. 'Let's call it a night,' she stated, then excused herself. 'I'll be back,' she said. To need to pee is a contagious feeling; I followed Gabby to not be left alone with Alice.

I entered the loo, Gabby had her face close to the slab

near the wash basin. 'I would have offered some to you but you are too vanilla,' she said with a hint of a patronizing attitude.

'It's late, we have a big day tomorrow,' Gabby said upon returning. 'You want us to drop you?' she asked.

'No, I am fine,' I confirmed.

'It's all right. Alice lives close to you, you girls can take the same cab,' she insisted and I reluctantly agreed. I had a quarter glass of margarita left. At first, I thought of letting it go to waste but then finished it in one go—what could one sip do which three drinks already did not?

8

The Contest

Ben

'*I*nvitations to chefs and critics—check, to friends of Bellissimo—check, customers who gave us harsh reviews—check, and to five random people—check,' I tallied it in my head, ensuring that I did not miss anyone for this elaborate tasting event. The invitations were hand-written and couriered along with an attractive gift hamper. Later, I followed up with the invitees over a WhatsApp message or a formal call, depending on how valuable their opinion was to us. If one thought lobbying does not work in the food and beverage industry like it works in politics or entertainment, then one is highly mistaken. Through his Gatsby*esque* social life, Arun was well acquainted with some established food columnists and chefs, well enough to invite them for an 'off the record' lunch and seek their candid opinion on how the new set menus would fare among epicures and proletarians alike. The event was also a filter to mellow any negative reviews and augment the positive ones when the official rollout would happen.

We were closed for walk-ins; the invitees would be served by both the chefs from their competing cuisines. The guests were free to only write about the version they liked or break it down into granular details, as was expected from the critics and aficionados. Arun too would probe some of his trusted peers for a conversational critique.

'Ben! Where's Sita?' Khan Chacha inquired restlessly. I had not seen her but reassured him that she would be here soon.

'Table eight to sixteen are reserved for the friends of Bellissimo,' I heard Philip instructing one of the serving staff. The veteran manager with his brooding persona and deep baritone reminded me of the character, Charles Carson, from the British television drama, *Downton Abbey*. In the cockles of my heart, I dreaded being like him—a man of proper manners but with a miserable mismatch between his refined tastes and dire fortunes. 'Mr Gower,' as most of us referred to him, was a proponent of this concept called 'Friends of Bellissimo,' a term he himself had coined and Arun had taken a liking to. In reality, these friends were a group of unrelated people who either had faith in Arun's endeavour all those years ago, had been avid ambassadors of Bellissimo's food or were friends of Arun and Natasha with a refined palate, which in their social circle pretty much everyone had or claimed to have.

The guests were to arrive in two hours and Sita was still not here. Now, I too was panicking. I tried her phone several times; it was switched off. Sita and Gabby were the focal points of both the tasting menus and since these dishes were not officially inducted in the main offering of the restaurant, there was no way for the other chefs to follow a written recipe and execute it flawlessly.

'All set?' Arun walked in with infectious energy. I could

not tell him about the soup we were in; I informed Chacha that she was still untraceable.

'Send someone to her house. I'll manage this,' Khan Chacha assured. I felt sorry for the old man; he had gone beyond his call of duty to mentor Sita so she could find a footing in this kitchen, and now, at this critical hour, he had to cover for her. At the same time, I was far more worried for Sita; she was not here and something was not right.

'Kathy, Chris, Nick ... I need a favour,' Khan Chacha requested with great hesitation.

'Pizza Contadina,' Gabby inquired on another station.

'Ready!' Dino responded. The two then started conversing in Italian before moving on to a final tally of their menu. That pizza looked heavenly with parmesan, prosciutto and unevenly sprinkled fresh basil.

'Pasta Fagioli, Ribollita, Polenta, Porceddu?' She checked and Alice, Mario and Jason responded in unison. While Alice and Mario were serving Gabby, Jason and Ryan were shared resources between her and Khan Chacha. Jason was rolling a whole suckling pig over a grill and Mario was regularly checking it for doneness. On the other station, the situation was no less than a nightmare—Khan Chacha, Kathy and Ajmal, along with Nick and Chris, were scrambling to put together Sita's menu, which they all knew in part but not in full—like an orchestra without its conductor.

'Sita?' Arun came in and asked.

'She isn't answering, I've sent the driver,' I explained and his rage had reached its end. He murmured something. I bet it was so profane he did not want to utter it out loud. The driver called to inform me that Sita was not at her Herne Hill residence and he was not able to communicate with Hira Lal.

'Call the authorities, inform them about a missing person,' Khan Chacha suggested after assuming what the driver had told me. Arun nodded in agreement.

'Should we cancel?' Arun asked but Khan Chacha refused. Honour for Khan Chacha was the essence of his life; he would be the last person to quit in a situation like this.

'See if she's fine,' he patted my shoulder and went back to working with his staff, preparing the meal in the final few minutes before the doors were to open.

'Didn't Sita come?' Alice came and asked; she and her team were almost done with their preparations.

'No, have you seen her?' I asked.

'Yeah, she had a drink with us last night—more than one actually,' she said with ample modulation, like she was auditioning for a low budget television drama.

'She was wonky, approaching strangers and we were afraid she'd end up with wrong company, so I took her to my house,' she detailed, now loud enough so everyone could hear.

'I woke her up in the morning but she was hammered out of her wits, had one too many! Let me call my flatmate and see if she's awake,' she said.

'Let it be,' enforced Khan Chacha.

I am certain that he did not believe her words, but even in broad strokes if what she had said was true—it was enough for Chacha to not depend on Sita. Everyone continued with the preparation, there was an unbearable silence on the floor, which was only amplified by the noise of meal preparations.

❦

Sita

'*How did I get here?*' I wondered in a dazed and confused state, like an animal tranquillised and waking up in a cage. The surroundings were unfamiliar and thumbnails from last night resurfaced to bring back some coherence.

The clock said it was 11.30 a.m., I jolted out of the bed and instinctively entered a door assuming it to be the bathroom. I could not recognise the person in the mirror. I washed my face repeatedly, hoping to see the face which would comfort me. I dug my face in the basin and drank from the tap. Then, I squeezed some toothpaste directly from the tube into my mouth and rinsed thoroughly, took a deodorant lying on the shelf and sprayed it all over me like a farmer sprays pesticides over his crop.

'Good morning. Care for an avo-toast?' A girl seated on the dining table asked. I had hurriedly gathered my belongings, all of which still stank of stale food and alcohol, and rushed out. The other girl was taking a fitness class via a video call.

'No thanks. How do I get to the Oxford Circus?' I asked impatiently.

'From the main door turn left. The tube station is half a mile out,' she said. I was running on the street. The snow did not make matters easy. I tripped and fell, gathered myself and ran again, making the passers-by look up from their phone screens and take fleeting notice of the rush I was in.

Once on the train, I wanted to text Khan Chacha and Baba. The battery was dead and there was no charging point in sight. I thought of asking someone to lend me their phones but none of the numbers were memorised. I was now at the mercy of time to see what would happen.

By the time I reached the restaurant, lunch had already begun. Everyone was busy with the preparations and plating. I saw Alice and Gabby working across the counter and wanted to slap them. I probably would have done that if I had not deserved that slap more. I approached Chacha meekly; he was instructing Kathy. The second course was being plated.

'I can help ...' I hesitatingly offered.

'GET OUT!' he yelled. Everyone froze for a moment. His face was red with rage, veins jutting out of his forehead and eyes welling up in anger and disappointment. I too was crying; my knees were shaking involuntarily. Ben tried to approach me but I rushed out of the kitchen.

Ben

It was a part of Bellissimo folklore that Khan Chacha had this intimidating persona, which everyone dreaded. They often wondered what would happen if he were to lose his cool one day? Well, today was that day and his roar felt like an avalanche—not only on the kitchen floor but even outside. Sita had rushed out and Arun and Philip rushed in to check if everything was all right. Gathering his cool, Khan Chacha went back to work. There was a commitment to fulfil and guests to serve; he would not be humiliated further.

I signalled to Arun that Sita was outside and he dashed out. I too stepped out of the kitchen to find a proper spot for myself with the guests. Unlike the other staff, I could come in any attire I liked and I chose the fern-coloured suede blazer I had ordered when I went with Arun to his tailor at Savile Row. Philip gave me a scornful look, insinuating I should not be here, but I did not intend to serve from the side-lines for the rest of my life. Natasha was also on this elite list of guests as the co-owner of the holding company that ran Bellissimo. She was still involved in the key decisions around the restaurant. She had brought her date along; after his stint as a rugby player ended, Diljeet ran a furniture shop and supplied furniture to Bellissimo before Arun's marriage and his vendor contract were annulled pretty much around the same time.

I joined them at the table, Natasha held my hand and asked, 'How are you, Ben?' She always greeted me with a genuine sense of warmth, and though we shared a rather odd relation—she was the ex-wife of my current boss—I still found a natural sense of comfort in her company. There weren't many people in the world I could call a friend but she certainly was one of them and that's what friends are for—they are like carbs, they are supposed to comfort you.

Looking around, I could see the obsessive footprints of Arun's painstaking inspection of the place. The distance between the chairs had been measured by a ruler, the napkin and name cards were kept at the exact angle for all the guests; he probably had spent all of last night choreographing who would sit where and would have sent the seating order to Philip in the morning. The flowers on each tabletop were fresh from the garden and manicured to perfection; the live piano bound the atmosphere together. We made small talk before getting down to the event, of which Natasha knew little about. What came to me as a surprise was that she was unaware of Sita's existence until now.

'Is it some desperate attempt to get back at Tony?' she asked.

'I don't think so,' I said, explaining the circumstances under which we met Sita and how her food was beyond comparison. Diljeet expressed he was now curious to try what she makes, but I had to break the insider news to them that Sita would not be cooking because of an embarrassing no-show.

'Is she all right? Should we postpone?' Natasha suggested. I told her that Khan Chacha was not willing to cancel the event and bring disgrace to Bellissimo.

The moment of reckoning was finally here. Servers from the kitchen started coming with dishes from both the menus— the wine and bread baskets were identical. Moving on, we got two distinct cheese boards. Gabby had played it safe with traditional cheese and classic Italian cold cuts but the other board was a complete mess. Why were we even having this competition if Sita was not cooking? The plating on her boards missed the mark and upon tasting the cheese, they lacked the harmony with which she would have arranged them.

'What are they doing?' Diljeet asked Natasha, referring to some food critics who were eating the cheese like rats nibbling on their bait in a trap, cautiously measuring how much they could eat without the gate closing in on them.

'Making notes,' she said, getting the sarcasm in his tone. 'Should we?'

'Just shut up and eat,' she punched him in his ribbed torso.

I loved these two together. She was the co-owner of this restaurant and he had no qualms about being at her ex-husband's event—they were enjoying their time like two teenagers out on a fast-food date.

'Is that …?' Diljeet asked.

'Yes, stop salivating,' Natasha confirmed, referring to actor Emily Blunt, a childhood friend of Arun's. When the soups came, Gabby's Tuscan Ribollita was perfection in a bowl.

'Isn't it a bit too messy for a fine diner?' Diljeet asked, referring to the Tuscan soup.

'It's supposed to be like this. This recipe is from the Middle Ages. The servants would take leftover bread from their master's dinner table and boil it to make a potage for themselves,' Natasha explained. I cherished these titbits of trivia; they made for interesting conversations in whatever little social life I could afford outside my unending office hours.

'But why would the rich pay a lot of money to eat what the poor ate?' he asked in jest and Natasha just gave him that look, one which would make you fall in love with her if you already hadn't. After finishing our measured portions, we sampled the other soup. The Kulith Minestrone. It was nowhere close to the first one in presentation or taste.

'I'm sure this isn't how it's supposed to be,' Natasha said after taking a sip. This was a one-sided contest from the word Go. Khan Chacha was a legendary butcher but not a chef, and the rest of the chefs were masters of their stations, but they did not have an artist's edge. Only a head chef could bring that to the board. I looked around to confirm if the other guests felt the same. Some had satiated expressions while others were camouflaging an unsavoury shock; it wasn't difficult to say who was having which soup. Arun was speaking with some of his trusted chefs and critics while they were eating.

'This was a mistake, all of it,' Arun sent me a text.

I looked at him from across the room and for the first time, I felt he acknowledged his defeat. Those eyes which had the eternal shine of optimism were now clouded with regret—we had a lapse in judgement about Sita.

In the last hour or so, it became clearer to me that we all stand on a narrow ladder of our present, with our toes twinkling restlessly to climb the rung ahead, but our heels shivering with the fear of the dark abyss which lies beneath. With each step upward, a new rung and a new abyss emerges, and the nature of our abyss is as unique as our fingerprints. For Philip, he was holding on to his ladder, cautious to not fall into the creek of irrelevance but also resistant to let anyone climb higher when he could not. For Natasha, Arun was her void with a strong gravitational pull and she was laughingly holding on to Diljeet to preserve the new ground she had created for herself. I too found a seat on this table, taking a tiny step into the upper echelons of society, emerging from a long-drawn-out and dysfunctional social void of embracing my identity during my formative years. Gabby too was doing all she could to achieve what she wanted, which unfortunately led Sita to slip into her own dark abyss.

'*What a waste of that immense potential,*' I sympathised with this promising young girl who had once blown our minds with her unique food.

Sita

I found refuge behind the same car in the back alley to keep out of Arun's sight. First, he called out my name, looked around, smoked his cigarette while waiting for me, but then he went in. I cried—first a lot, then a little and then, more

... and a lot more—till I had drained out all the self-loathe for what had happened last night. My cheeks were freezing; I could feel a burning sensation from the warm trail the tears had left. My throat was dry and my lips were clipped together. Familiar sights of the broken window glass, leaking pipe and chipping paint gave me a sense of deja vu. I asked myself: *'Ten years from now, what will I make of this very moment? Is escaping the answer?'*

'The biggest regret in life is not failure but not following your dreams,' I recalled the words of the old lady who used to live near our village and would sing at the crossroads. Such was the melody in her voice that the passers-by would stop and listen to her. My uncle, the local constable, had to request her to sing in a bazaar and not on the road to avoid the traffic jams she was attracting. One afternoon, while walking back from the school I stopped at a bakery for some patties—that is where I first heard her sing.

'Who is she?' I asked the baker.

'God knows! She comes here every day and sings all day! What a nuisance,' he ranted. After she had finished singing, I approached her.

'Your voice is so melodious,' I complimented and she smiled with a twinkle in her eyes, which rested within those wrinkled and baggy sockets. We were sitting on the stone slab in the bazaar. It was a busy autumn day. I offered her a patty; at first, she was hesitant but then, she took it.

'What's your name?' she asked.

'Sita.'

'I had a friend called Sita,' she said while looking into the distance. She did not mention anything else about her friend and was mumbling things to herself.

'Do you live nearby?' I asked.

'I live nowhere.'

Her eccentricity was not just limited to her appearance. Wearing a brown wool robe, a Himachali cap with tribal jewellery, she was from one of the nearby settlements of herdsmen.

'Where did you learn to sing?' I asked and she just smiled at me without giving an answer.

'Will you teach me?' I asked curiously.

'What will you give me in return?' she asked. I was confused, was she seeking money? I could offer some after speaking with Baba.

'How much will you take?' I asked.

'Everything you have,' her eccentricity was rapidly escalating towards insanity.

'Will you give it? Will you? Everything you have?' she repeated fanatically and then went quiet like we had never been having a conversation at all.

'How old are you?' she asked calmly.

'Fifteen.'

'What an age to be. Ask an old person and they will readily exchange their regrets with failure,' she said. 'Singing is not your calling, something else is, something for which you are willing to give your everything. And what that is, is for you to find. Remember child, the biggest regret in life is not failure but not following your dreams, not making that attempt. And you don't come to regret it until your life is almost over,' she placed a hand on my cheek and spoke these words. She got up and resumed singing a Gaddi[44] song of her people.

---

[44]Gaddi: Tribe in Himachal Pradesh

I never saw her again, but I never forgot what she had said.

I think there were two versions of me. The first accepted things easily and the second did not accept the first version. In what was increasingly becoming a habitual boost to propel myself out of such tides of self-doubt, I stood up and paced across the ally and swung the door open into the kitchen. Everyone stopped upon seeing me. But the thing with confidence is that it is an aeroplane and your fears are the runway. First you have to overcome them to take off, and then they help you land safely. And the doubts others have about you? They are nothing more than cars on the road, they will appear big and noisy as long as you are on the ground, but they can never get in your path. The higher you go, the less relevant they become. Khan Chacha was still fuming. Rightly so, I had made a mistake. We all do. But I would not let it get in my way of becoming who I was supposed to be. As a girl who grew up without a mother, the only thing I heard from the people was—'girls belong in the kitchen.'

'Well, this Sita certainly belongs in the kitchen and she will own it!' I told myself.

'Kathy! Bring the spaghetti. Chris, fetch the morels,' I called out, taking command of my menu. The third course— Primi was underway and the Secondi was yet to be served. I was in no mood to let this moment slip away from me. I inspected the Nihari Ossobuco which Khan Chacha was struggling to plate. I took over. Seeing my resolve, he did not object.

'Be original,' I whispered to myself and placed the cream-coloured risotto on the plate. I tasted some off the ladle. It lacked that hint of spices that gave it its depth and invoked that distinctly Indian flavour. I discarded the two plates I had already served it on and went to the vessel where the risotto was. Ideally, I would have infused the spices while cooking, but right now, I had to come up with a hack. I started heating oil in a saucepan and added powdered nutmeg and cinnamon to it. I poured warm water into a cup and infused it with strands of saffron. Once the cinnamon and nutmeg oil started bubbling, it went straight into the risotto vessel. I stirred it till it was mixed evenly. Then I started laying the risotto on the plates—first ... second ... third ... fourth ... there were fifty more to go. Kathy was swift to take over, it allowed me the time to spray the saffron infused water onto the risotto with an atomizer.

'We're running out of time,' Philip came in and panicked, adding more stress to a situation which already felt like a pressure cooker with a clogged whistle. Khan Chacha brought in the lamb shanks. Traditionally, Ossobuco is done with veal shanks for tenderness and by replacing the veal with lamb, it acquired that signature touch of the Indian dish, the Nihari.

'Ryan, fried onions please!' I asked the sauté chef and he was on it in no time. Thankfully, Nick had chopped them in advance.

'Oh shit! The Aglio Olio!' I panicked and went to check the pasta. Thankfully, after Kathy had finished with plating the risotto, she had moved on to plate the spaghetti as well.

'Chris!' I shouted and he promptly handed me the morels. I had too many balls in the air while running from counter to counter.

'They should stay hidden beneath the spaghetti,' I demonstrated to Kathy. She felt encouraged to take on more responsibility than she was used to.

I came back to the Ossobuco and started placing the

shanks on the risotto; this was something I had to do myself for all the plates. There was a certain way to angle the rust-coloured lamb shank, resting partly against and partly on the risotto, with a few strands of saffron and fried onions for the garnish. This was when the plate became the canvas, and food, the art! I had never prepared so many identical looking dishes in one go. I tasted one, it was not perfect; in my practice days I had made it better but for now this was the best I could do.

'Service!' I called with a sense of relief. The dishes went out, first the pasta and then, the Ossobuco—waiting for board exam results felt less tense. The remaining courses also followed, thankfully, they did not require much preparation.

We had a few minutes of exhale time after the last course went out. I walked up to Khan Chacha. He was standing aloof. I stood there with my head down, held my ears with a genuine sense of guilt for what I had put him through but he ignored me and went out.

Philip entered the kitchen, 'Mr Mehra is asking for the entire staff.'

Everyone looked at each other with unnerving anticipation. Having depleted my dose of adrenaline while plating, I was now among the last in the queue. Most guests had left, but some still lingered on. At the door, Arun was giving that odd cheek-to-cheek kiss to one English actress; I had seen her a lot but I didn't know her name. *'He really is rich and famous,'* I thought. Then a smart Indian woman and a Sikh man greeted Arun and left.

'She is Natasha, Arun's wife—well ex-wife now, and the tall hunk with her, Diljeet Maan, her boyfriend. Don't blame yourself if you can't get it, sometimes even I don't,' Ben whispered. Arun being divorced did not come as a surprise, he seemed that way. He had not done something specific or revealed it in any of our conversations but intuitively when I tried to imagine his background and life—Arun being divorced was a natural impulse.

The last two guests who stayed back were Marco Russo and Graham Reed!

'Are they really here!' I freaked out. They were chatting with each other and laughing. 'How?' I thought, 'Aren't they jealous of each other? Aren't they rivals?' Arun came back and asked us to gather near them.

'Thank you for the lovely experience,' he said.

'Today, I invited some of our most trusted patrons to vote for the menu they liked, but more importantly, for the menu they'd be willing to pay for,' he announced and then he called out to Philip who was counting votes from a ballot.

'We have a verdict,' Philip said and paused. I could hear my heartbeat.

'Indo-Italian fusion—eleven votes,' he declared and Alice chuckled.

'Cucina Povera—forty-two votes—'

Alice and the others started cheering, interrupting Philip.

'—seems like we have a clear winner,' he asserted.

'I guess we do,' said Arun. 'But I have with me two good friends who are here to weigh in on the finer aspects of our menus. They are legends of the kitchen and I won't belittle them with an introduction,' he said and looked at Russo.

'Thank you for your hospitality,' Russo said in his thick Italian accent.

'I won't mince words. The Indo-Italian fusion sounded absurd when Arun called me and it is a failure from the get go,' he stated. 'It's bastardization, it's sacrilegious; the whole concept of Indian-Italian fusion is wrong on the plate and wrong on the palate,' he spoke, landing his fist on the table and crushing my soul underneath. My eyes welled up. I was making my best effort to not let the tears flow. One of my idols had just told me that whatever I had done had been absolute rubbish.

'Cucina Povera,' he said, kissing his fingers with a slurpy sound. 'It made me travel for miles and in years, it took me to my home in Marche, to my childhood, in my mama's cucina. Priceless!' he said and came forward to kiss Gabby's hand. The two started speaking in Italian.

'You can't poach her, Marco!' Arun said in jest.

'Don't worry, that's exactly what I am telling her. I can't poach her but she is free to join me,' he replied and then he and Arun shared a fist bump. And then, Arun called Graham.

'I too have some feedback for you folks, and since I am famous, I pretty much have a license to cane you!' Graham said with a straight face. 'I was kidding,' he said and we lightened up. 'Or was I?' he said harshly.

'But seriously, this has been a good lunch. I may steal some recipes for my own restaurant,' he said—the man was an actor even outside his television shows.

'You dare,' Arun said laughingly.

'Full marks to the Cucina Povera; it preserves the most authentic version of Italian food. I would eat it any day I crave for Italian,' Graham said and everyone congratulated Gabby.

'From the Indo-Italian section, I will ignore everything— it was just confusion on a plate,' he added. I don't know if with each word I was becoming invisible or was being pushed naked under a spotlight. By now, the tears were involuntarily flooding from my eyes.

'But that Nihari Ossobuco and Himalayan Aglio Olio—it is stardust Arun, it is magic!' he said and my heart stopped beating for a moment—before it started pounding again.

'I don't know who made what, but I'm certain those two recipes came from someone special. The thing with food is that it never remains constant, and it never should! Experimentation leads to evolution. While the purists may argue that this Indo-Italian fusion is blasphemy, who the hell are we to decide? And who the fuck cares as long as it tastes good? And that's what people pay for—simple food that tastes good,' he said, bringing my hopes back from a ventilator.

'But—' Marco interrupted.

'My friend, I respect you, but I don't agree with you,' said Graham. 'The way those two dishes were plated—none of that microgreens and flower bullshit—we don't need to fit every cuisine within the French preconceptions for it to be gourmet. Your Indo-Italian menu is a risk Arun, but it's a risk worth taking,' he concluded.

'I invited you both to make my job easier!' Arun said sarcastically and while everyone laughed, I was in no mood to react. My dreams were oscillating like a pendulum, at one end being crushed beneath brutal rejection and at the other end being cheered by praise; all while being strung from a thin thread of hope.

'Warriors, we shall take your leave,' Graham called out to everyone; he downed his leftover sparkling water and went out with Russo and Arun.

'It's okay, it's over. You did your best,' Gabby came forward and offered a handshake. I was not in a space to respond.

The main door opened again, flushing the room with

natural light and a silhouette of a man rolled in a wheelchair—
an old lady was seated on it. She had a grace on her face
which could only be earned by experiencing all the emotions
there were to experience, and then, elevating oneself above
them all. Her skin, though wrinkled, had a sheen; if one
were to look closely in her eyes, one could see the past play
out like a black and white film. Her hair was grey and she
was wearing a shell-coloured salwar-kameez with a pashmina[45]
shawl, kundan[46] bangles and earrings; they looked antique.

'Khasmanukane[47], how could you forget me?' she scolded
Ben and gave him a gentle whack on his belly. She was
wheeled to a table. Ben came near me and whispered, 'Arun's
grandmother, she can be your wild card.'

'What do we have here ...' the grandmother interrogated
after picking up a menu lying on the table. She wore her
glasses, hung from her neck with a braided black chain and
she started reading through the tasting menu. Arun was back,
he came forward to touch his grandmother's feet and asked
her how she came to be here and she candidly complained
that Ben had forgotten to invite her.

'Good you are here, Dadima. I really need your guidance,'
Arun requested.

'Would you get me the Tuscan Ribollita, the Kulith
Minestrone and then Himalayan Aglio Olio and Pasta Fagioli?'
she ordered two dishes from each menu.

'Actually, replace the Aglio Olio with the Haak Ravioli,'
she told Philip. The woman knew her food. She had ordered

---

[45]Pashmina: Fabric made of rare wool
[46]Kundan: Traditional gold and gemstone work
[47]Khasmanukane: Silly

dishes which resembled each other to a great degree, yet one could feel the distinction in their flavours and inspiration. With that, the chefs went in to prepare her order.

This was the bleak chance I had been seeking to redeem myself and I would not make a mess of it.

The mise en place was already done and it took us ten minutes to cook the soup and pasta.

'Service!' I called out and Ben came in.

'I think you should take it yourself,' he suggested in a low voice. I took his advice. Seeing me, Gabby, who had just handed her order to the serving staff, also took over and came out. We served the food and the old lady started to sample it. She ate with the same grace she embodied.

'The Ribollita is delicious,' she complimented Gabby. She had a couple more spoons before she cleansed her palate and sampled the Kulith Minestrone.

'What's your name, beta?' she asked me.

'Sita,' I responded modestly.

'This Kulith reminds me of home,' she said. 'I am a mountain girl; this city life has changed my ways but not my soul.' She extended a hand to hold mine. Though her hands barely had muscles and the bones could be felt beneath paper-thin skin, her grip was firm—not threatening or brooding—but firm with a zest for life.

'My apologies, I may not be able to finish all of this,' she said with a gentle smile and took a piece of Ravioli and a bite from the Pasta Fagioli.

'I now understand your dilemma,' she told Arun. 'To choose between two goods isn't a blessing to have.'

She thanked Gabby and me for making the food for her and then turned to Arun.

'You must not deprive the people of this food,' she said, referring to Gabby's meal. 'Outside this kitchen, this food is only available in Italy. But here, what this little girl has done by blending Indian and Italian flavours—it does not exist anywhere else but in your restaurant,' she said. 'This food is a memory, an experience and that, my child, should be your new highlight.'

'Congratulations! You just won!' Ben whispered while squishing my hand tightly. I was still processing her feedback. Would Arun take the word of his grandmother above everything else that had happened today?

9

The Making of a Dream

Sita

'We can't call it Indian-Italian fusion, it needs a sobriquet,' Audrey said, referring to the set-menu.

The fortyish English woman was the boss of the creative agency tasked with the relaunch of Bellissimo. Arun, Ben and I were in the conference room that had a long table with a generous spread of biscuits, mini-croissants and sandwiches to accompany our morning beverages. The glass walls of the high-floor room overlooked the London skyline; the sun had come out after a week.

It had been two days since the tasting challenge and I still could not believe I had won; the feeling was more of relief than triumph. I guess such is with all endeavours, which, at the onset seem beyond one's grasp, but minute by minute, inch by inch, one gets closer to realising what once felt impossible.

'Intalian?' A young man from the agency proposed and Audrey gave him a look equivalent to a tight slap.

All of us, except her, were seated; her blue business suit

and five feet ten stature dominated the room. Ben and I had taken a taxi to this place while Arun had reached directly. On the way, Ben told me that Audrey and Arun had briefly dated and since then, have remained work friends with the provision of being each other's booty call. Through most of the meeting I was aghast imagining how one could meaningfully focus on work with someone you see naked on a casual basis?

'We have some data for you, a focused group survey,' she said. 'It captures the customers' perception of Bellissimo.' She then prompted her team member to project the slides, and another person started to read them out loud.

'Gourmet—four people, Star rated—eight people, Italian—ten, Overrated—three people, Spaghetti in Box—four, Expensive—six, Arun Mehra—five people, Anthony Dellucci—seven people,' he read out, elocuting each word; the last name made the agency boss rather awkward in front of Arun. I guess their fallout must be public knowledge.

'Mr Mehra, we need a narrative—a relaunch alone won't create the buzz, it needs a story!' Audrey swiftly changed the topic and subtly signalled her team member to switch the slide projecting Anthony's name. Arun nodded, willing to move past the unsavoury moment.

'So ... when did you think of becoming a chef?' the girl sitting next to me asked.

'Ever since I was a child. Ten I guess ...' I said.

'And you haven't learnt how to cook?'

'Not formally.'

'Please don't mind the questions. How did you develop your skills?' she asked and I told them an abridged version of the same story I had told Arun in Himachal and included the recent crash course Khan Chacha had given me.

'This! Right there, this is the narrative! You are an embodiment of passion and will, an icon for those who dream,' said Audrey.

'What exactly are you proposing?' asked Arun.

'Mr Mehra, give us a week. Now we know what to do. Sita, we'll come down for a meal, my team will trouble you for more details,' she concluded. Ben probed her for executional details, emphasizing that we had to launch the new menu by the start of spring.

'Don't worry, our PR and media-buying teams are on standby. Once we nail the core concept, they'll follow the lead,' Audrey reassured Ben. She walked us to the elevator.

In the lift, Arun received a message. The smirk on his face made me wonder if it was Audrey. 'Let's have lunch?' Arun asked when we were out on the street. Was it a question or a statement remained unclear but both Ben and I agreed.

I had been in London for two months but it felt like two years—one thing that had not changed was the cold. The city was partly covered in snow, heaps of flakes were gathered round the street lamps and were scattered on the rooftops, and the road was striped like a zebra. We stepped into a heritage building with two flags hung from its facade. It was a members-only club.

'The Oxford and Cambridge Club,' Ben whispered and Arun led us inside the coffee room, which actually was a restaurant. With mahogany ply on the walls, large paintings and dark wooden tables, this place suited Arun's persona. We placed our orders. I opted for a braised duck with a pomegranate reduction while Ben and Arun ordered steaks. The room was filled with young and old men—the odd lady here and there.

'Brace yourself, life as you know is about to change forever,' Arun said.

'I don't get you.'

My life had already changed the moment I had got on the plane, what else could be that drastic? Both Arun and Ben laughed like they knew something I did not.

'My love, you're gonna be a star,' Ben said with a smile. I did not understand what they meant, not until the following few days when my notion of time and peace went into a blender and were mixed till nothing remained of them.

Every day, I was doing ten other things apart from cooking.

'Let's get rid of the split ends,' the hair stylist mumbled. It was a weekday afternoon, I was out to get a haircut when I should have been cooking lunch for our guests. Ben was deputed to accompany me.

'Dutch braid or Chignon?' the stylist asked.

'Too bold,' said Ben.

'Space buns?'

'Golly no!' Ben freaked. The stylist showed us four more styles and Ben nodded in the negative.

'This one,' I intervened and confirmed the French braid from the brochure. It wasn't different from how I did my hair.

'But, Sita, it won't be a makeover!' Ben said.

'It doesn't need to be,' I asserted. I was in no mood or need for a change and henceforth, only I would decide what worked for me.

'Madame, would you like to try our new organic detox facial rejuvenation?' the stylist recommended it and I confirmed.

'I don't mind that as well,' Ben followed. We had our faces smeared with a green paste and were also getting a pedicure done; that was Ben's idea.

After our ninety-minute haul at the barber shop, we grabbed a shawarma from the street and headed to Harvey & Sons, Arun's personal tailors on Savile Row, who also designed the outfit for Bellissimo's staff. They were regular tailors but Arun had persuaded them to design his restaurant's uniform.

'What about a traditional double-breasted coat?' the fifty-plus tailor suggested; his apprentice brought the coats for a trial. The store reminded me of the movie, *The Kingsmen*, which I had watched on the flight. This coat was too old fashioned and serious and the tailor read my rejection.

'The Venetian? It's our signature with a tapered and overlapping lapel—quite popular these days,' he said, showing us a grey-coloured short jacket, identical to the one Gabby wore. Even though I really liked this one, I did not want to imitate her.

'Some young chefs are just going for a casual t-shirt with a denim apron,' he suggested. The store lent me a t-shirt to try on. Though an apron was associated with a junior rank in our kitchen hierarchy, from the moment I put it on, this apron and tee allowed me to be myself; there was no pretence in this unlike the formal coats. I was free from the burden of earning my place in the kitchen. I saw myself in the mirror and that was it, I had found my armour.

'May I suggest clubbing it with this?' Ben put a baseball cap on my head; it matched the look.

'Clothes?' he asked while we were having our tea and coffee at Starbucks.

'What about them?'

'Let's get your chic!' he stated and we took the rest of the day to shop. After months of indecisiveness, I finally bought a pair of jeans.

'Take two at least,' Ben insisted.

Along with the jeans, I also bought t-shirts, jackets and sweaters. I was finally getting used to the London way of dressing. Four days later, when my new aprons arrived, I didn't wear them to the kitchen!

'Make an X with the whisk and spatula,' instructed the photographer. Ben had brought us to a photo studio after Audrey had asked him to. I was wearing a black t-shirt, jeans, my denim apron and a cap.

'Smile! That's too much, no—it doesn't look real. Just keep a straight face. Let's try a couple of variations—one pose with the knife, use the big one. Now a close up, dab! That makeup is too much. Let's take a break ...'

The puppetry lasted for four hours.

All this while, I was also working with an image consultant Audrey had recommended. The girl was barely older than me and yet she shadowed me wherever I went. 'Take control of your movements. Don't enter a place and start looking around, let others look at you. Always have a soft smile, not too wide, you have to be humble but firm in everything you do and say ...' she gave me a textbook worth of do's and don'ts to remember.

That evening I was back at the restaurant after four days. I went straight to Khan Chacha who was carving out a steak. I bought a muffler for him.

'What's this?' he asked. I requested he open it. We stepped aside from the workstation.

'Does this undo everything?' he remarked after seeing the muffler.

'No, but it can lead to a fresh start,' I said. 'I know I've let you down, embarrassed you in front of everyone. I made a mistake. I am sorry; there's nothing more I have to say.'

'Let it be,' he said, placing his hand on my shoulder. 'Your menu releases soon, take this time to master everything. Remember, perfection is a quest to reach the horizon,' he said. I had truly missed his tips and motivation.

'And if you need anything, I'll be at my station,' he reassured. He looked tired, depleted from exhaustion but he also had a sense of relief on his face, he had done the impossible, taken a backyard cook and given her the wings to fly in this culinary world. And now, he sat like an old eagle, after the youngling had left the nest.

Ben

'What's this?' Arun asked. Gabby did not offer a response. She had just barged into his office and stamped an envelope on the desk.

'I'm not accepting it,' he said without opening it.

'Please ...' Gabby said helplessly. Pity was not a word I thought I would associate with this woman who I often described to others as a formidable kitchen ninja.

'There's nothing here for me to stay ...'

'That's not true, Gabby, we need you.'

'For what? To take orders from a rookie? Who'll tell me how to cook the food of my own people?'

'No! You will ...'

'No Arun, I am out,' she interrupted him.

'Actually, you can't go. You signed a two-year lock in and no compete, so unless you plan to work in a different industry ...' I began.

'That won't be needed,' Arun overruled, reached out for his drawer, took out Gabby's contract and tore it in front of her.

'I won't hold you back because of a piece of paper. You are free. But remember that feeling, when we won the star? Felt on top of the world?' Arun ignited the most memorable moment of our professional lives.

It was during my first year here and Gabby's second. Arun had found through his connections that we were getting a star, but we didn't believe it until it happened and when it did, we had the wildest bender.

'Chug! Chug! Chug! Chug!' the room was shouting in chorus. Gabby and Arun were the last ones standing in the beer chugging competition. I had quit after my second—most went to sixth and one random bloke from the serving staff touched double digits, but for the past five pints, Gabby and Arun were in a deadlock. When the sixteenth mugs of ale were placed on the table, everyone thought Gabby would fall. They took their mugs, and on the count of three started chugging; halfway through, one of them snorted the beer out of their nostrils and fell to the floor. Gabby was the last one standing, she outdrank Arun!

Standing in his office, the three of us imagined the same moment; coming back to reality, Gabby's resignation was still on the table.

'You didn't lose to Sita, at best it was a tie. You know it. Your food is the gold standard, but the Indo-Italian food is our best chance to disrupt things and make a mark again,'

Arun said. Gabby didn't respond but her guard was down, she was softening up.

'The Sunday brunch will also be revamped—we'll serve the Cucina Povera,' he offered. She looked at him, 'That is, if you decide to stay ...'

'I want a promotion. I've been filling in for Tony,' she demanded. 'I want Exec Chef.'

'Done!' said Arun. I was astonished by the ease with which he gave in, but Gabby was playing her cards right. Sita's food had an innovative edge, but this ship needed a captain, someone who could weather the storm and steam hard when the winds were favourable, a veteran who knew the minutiae of the daily drills of a kitchen. That's where Gabby was indispensable, at least for the moment.

'And twenty per cent more salary than he had been drawing,'

'Ten,' Arun countered and she agreed.

She was making more than double of what she had ten minutes back. I secretly regretted never developing a liking for the culinary arts.

'And *she* reports to whom?'

'I don't need to tell you, Gabby. They all report to you. My only request is that you give Sita a space for experimentation and guide her with the overall aesthetic our food stands for,' Arun concluded. They both arrived at an agreement and exchanged a nod instead of a handshake. Like the wordsmith and diplomat he was, he had managed to retain Gabby.

'That was a close one,' I said after she left.

'For the time. Remember Ben, as a business owner, you have money, designations and fame to reward your employees with—give these out generously but not all three in one go.

Gabby got the first two, but Sita will become our face,' he said and lit a cigarette.

'And keep these in a safe,' he added, handing me a pile of contracts; Gabby's was on top of the heap.

'I need a name, why are we still calling it Indo-Italian, where's Audrey?' he immediately returned to the matter at hand. I texted her and she confirmed a meeting for the next day. We were ten days away from the relaunch.

'Blitzkrieg,' said Audrey; she and her team had come down to the restaurant.

'During your launch week, we will hijack traditional and social media in London and play Sita's story. It coincides with International Women's Day and that will give us a great boost,' she explained.

'And the media buying?' I asked, worried about our timelines and where we currently stood.

'Don't worry, we're a full-service agency. The stills are in the can, the buying and digital teams are on standby,' assured Audrey. I could not help but marvel at the hollow repetition of her words.

'What are we naming this cuisine?' asked Arun. He was on the edge of his patience. He trusted me with the fine print execution of the campaign, but for him, it was important to know what we were offering.

'La Sinfonia Indiana ... the Indian Symphony,' Audrey evoked these names rather dramatically, expecting a thunderous applause but none were impressed.

'And ...?' Arun asked. 'I'm sure you have options?'

He had the agency on the defensive; they had thought they would have just uttered the words and we would have printed them on our menu.

'We do …' Audrey said unconfidently and her team began throwing words, hoping something would stick. 'Bella Donna', 'Indiana', 'Fusione Indiana', 'Espressione Indiana,' the barrage of terms began.

'Guys, stop reading from Google translate,' Arun yelled, visibly frustrated at the lack of work they had put into it.

'I still think "Intalian" is good,' the agency guy repeated his suggestion and this time Audrey's stare was not like a single slap but two tight ones.

'Sita's Kitchen,' a voice in the background uttered unsurely.

'Who's that?' I overheard Audrey ask her deputy in a hushed tone.

'A new intern,' replied her associate.

'What's that?' Arun asked.

'I think you should call your menu Sita's Kitchen,' a young girl of Asian descent came forward and said nervously. Audrey tried to silence her but Arun intercepted; he was now talking to the novice directly.

'Why?'

'The campaign strategy is to tell Sita's story—of a young girl, a self-taught maverick who is daring to conquer London with her food,' the apprentice said and then paused, assuming someone would challenge her. But no one did.

'Go on,' Arun insisted.

'You're right, the names we proposed were picked up from translation tools and the customers will catch it too,' she impressed everyone in the room with her honesty.

'If it is Sita's story and Sita's food, it should bear her name on the menu,' the young girl concluded.

'What's your name?' Arun asked.

'Lisa.'

'Thank you, Lisa. We have the menu name. Audrey, Ben—you know what to do. And one more thing. From now, Lisa will take the lead on our account,' Arun said and left.

Sita

'*Can reality be so good you fear that it's a dream?*' I was anxious, afraid that anytime now I would wake up in Himachal and go out to graze the sheep, forgetting this intricate vision of being a chef in London.

While waiting for the train on the platform I saw a large advertisement bearing my picture. People were walking past it, hardly taking notice, but in that moment, it did not matter; that ad was only placed for me. It was one of the many images clicked in the studio, but the background had been digitally altered from a white paper screen to a green graphic with subtle line drawings of the Colosseum and the Taj Mahal. The colour of my t-shirt and cap had been changed from black to white and I was given multiple hands, like Ma Durga; in each I was holding a tomato, a cheese slice, a spatula, a whisk, a book, a mobile, some uncooked spaghetti and a knife—all of which I had separately held during the photoshoot. My skin tone was much lighter, my cheeks were squeezed in like dried apricots and my lips and bust were enhanced, like how strawberries and apples look in pictures, attractive but unreal.

'Introducing Sita's Kitchen at *The* Bellissimo' read the board with an accompanying subtext, 'Progressive Italian

Fusion'. Scattered across the frame were also names of the dishes, which had made it to the final menu: Keema Lasagne, Himalayan Aglio Olio, Nihari Ossobuco with Saffron Risotto, Cashmere alla Caprese. They even had a one-line description of what the dishes were. At the bottom was the tagline. 'It sounds absurd till you taste it!'

While I stood marvelling at my own image, two trains had already come and left and it was only after the onslaught of the office-goers had thinned that a few people stopped to notice that the face on the wall was mine. The third train was arriving on the platform. *'I must board this to not get late,'* I told myself. The same ad was also at the Oxford Circus station when I got off; while walking to the restaurant, I saw it at a bus stand too. This really was a dream.

Today was the grand rollout. The kitchen felt like it was a new place, like everyone had changed. Standing in the same place, surrounded by the same people—I had even been through times when I had heard them giggle behind my back and ignore me on my face—but today, they all welcomed me with a warm applause.

'Best of luck,' Ryan was the first to congratulate. Kathy embraced me gently, 'At your service, Chef,' she said. As a part of the revamp, she was now to assist me.

Ben too gave me a tight hug.

'You deserve every bit of it ...' he said animatedly. Chris, Nick, Ajmal, Dino, Mario, Jason and Tom, they all came in and greeted me warmly.

'I'll see you in a bit,' Alice told Gabby and stepped out with a box of cigarettes in her hand. Gabby was standing at her station, and we finally made eye contact. I walked towards her with a slight bit of hesitation, which I hoped was not visible to the others. We stood at an arm's distance. There was a moment of silence. I was blank, unsure of how she would react. She reached towards her slab, took a package wrapped in a thin paper and unwrapped an apron from it. It was the same apron I had selected and it bore my name: 'Sita Pandit, Chef de Cuisine.' I was now the second in command!

'Congratulations,' she said and put the apron around my neck, turned me around and fastened it tightly.

'Water under the bridge?' she said while extending a handshake and a slight smile. I nodded and we shook hands, unanimously and perhaps unconsciously, everyone erupted in an applause.

Finally, Khan Chacha came forward and murmured a prayer, touching the prayer bead to my forehead; I had come full circle since that cold morning when we had begun training.

It was customary for the restaurant to be empty for the first half an hour after opening, but never before did that half hour feel like half a life. The gates were finally breached. The first customers for the day had come.

Curiosity got the better of me. I reached for the door separating the kitchen from the dining room and peeped in through the small glass window. Philip was talking to a young couple. A few more guests came in through the main door.

'They've ordered the set menu,' Gabby looked up from the screen. We had the mise en place ready and the next fifteen minutes were spent meticulously assembling the orders.

'First course for service,' said Dino, placing five bread baskets on the collection table.

'You focus on Primi and Secondi. I'll take care of the rest,' Gabby said. Between lunch and dinner, I made multiple batches of Kulith Minestrone, Nihari Ossobuco and Himalayan

Aglio Olio—and with each batch I was trying to maintain consistency but also pushing myself to make it better than the last one. Being busy has an unusual effect on time, the first few minutes of the morning felt like a double shift but the following hours finished within minutes, like how time lapses in a video.

'The customers want to meet you,' Philip came in and said. We had stopped taking orders for the night and the guests were on their last course. I stepped out, unsure why they wanted to see me, dreading that they would complain about how bad the food was.

'It's been our pleasure to eat this food,' a sophisticated couple complimented and shook my hands. 'We've never tasted something so good,' said a man from a group of working professionals, the others echoed his thoughts and then, a young woman in the group insisted I click a photo with them.

'Do you mind if I tag you on Insta?' she asked and I agreed. 'What's your handle?'

'"sitaskitchen"—without a space or apostrophe,' I told her. It was a new handle, created and co-managed by Lisa from Audrey's agency. The girl searched for me and tagged me; a couple of others did the same. The first day laid the blueprint for the weeks to come. Word of mouth and the social media buzz spread and we started attracting seekers of this unique menu.

'That bitch is growing claws,' Nick confided in me about what Alice had said to Gabby.

Her comment did not bother me, but I was pleased to know that Gabby had sternly asked Alice to focus on her work or get out of the kitchen. I was certain Gabby and Alice had spiked my drink, but my gullibility was as much at fault as their malice. I did not intend to be best friends with Gabby and would always watch my back around her, but I would be lying if I did not recognise the relief I felt in this newfound ally she had become. Our kitchen, which until a few days back was divided into two factions, had now come together for a singular cause. Every day, for every dish, we strived to make the experience memorable for our customers.

'Set menus for table four, seven, fifteen and twenty,' Gabby said and I was on the preparations. By now, I had delegated most tasks to the station chefs and I would step in to strike the right balance of flavours and do the final plating. Going out to the dining area during every meal had become a routine. I would check in with the customers about how the food was and most of the comments were favourable.

'Seventy per cent ordered the set menu,' Philip said, summing up the monthly report.

Ben, Philip and I were in Arun's office. Every day since the launch of the new menu was long and tiring, but extremely rewarding. It was my first of such meetings, usually Gabby would attend these, but today Arun had invited me instead.

'It's all organic,' said Ben, showing Arun and me his tablet screen. Our food was getting favourable ratings on various portals—most were between four and five out of five, with an odd two stars here and there.

'Unusually good! It's fusion done right; Unique flavours; The Nihari Ossobuco is a winner. Himalayan Aglio Olio is a vegan's delight; Progressive. Fusion. Excellent …'

The reviews raved on. It had been a month since we started serving the new menu. London had truly taken a liking to my cooking.

'I wasn't wrong after-all,' Arun proclaimed.

'Thank you,' I said courteously. I think he had expected me to thank him for this opportunity.

'Check with Audrey, has she secured the slot?' Arun asked Ben. Philip was struggling to hide his displeasure. He would never be convinced that this fusion food should be served, irrespective of its success or otherwise.

'Thank you, Mr Gower,' Arun said, sensing his discomfort and Philip left.

'That's great Audrey,' Ben said over the phone. 'Guess what?' he held my hands and started hopping, 'You, my love, have landed an interview with Olivia Hart!'

I had a blank expression on my face.

'Tell me you know her! You're half a Briton now!' he exclaimed. I was still clueless. 'Darling, the most admired lady on British television is about to take you live!'

I found myself in a television studio sooner than expected, the lights facing us were so bright, everything else appeared black. It was a Sunday morning. Arun and I were on the show, *Good Morning London*. The set had a giant LED behind us, which showed a panoramic image of the Thames and Westminster. Our interviewer and host, Olivia Hart was fiftyish, her foundation-clad face and shiny blonde hair looked artificial in person, but bewitching on screen. Arun was eating a dark chocolate while the makeup artist waited for him to finish—seeing the man standing, he handed the chocolate to Olivia and signalled for her to eat some.

'This is a first,' she mumbled smilingly, broke a small piece from the bar, ate it elegantly and kept the rest beneath her desk. She sipped some water, careful to not stain her lip colour, she then did a quick check in the mirror held by her makeup artist.

'And we go live in ten ... nine ... eight ...' the man behind the camera started prompting.

'Last week, I had dinner,' said Olivia, looking into the camera. The red light was on. 'What's remarkable about that? People have dinner every night. But last week I ate a meal that challenged my notions about food,' she added, speaking with such warmth as if someone was sitting inside the camera lens.

'London knows Bellissimo as a gem on its culinary map and recently they've been making news for a rather unusual menu by an extraordinary chef. To talk more about it I have with us, Arun Mehra, the owner of Bellissimo and Sita Pandit, the Himalayan wonder chef,' she said and asked us about what inspired us to blend Italian food with Indian.

'I call it my great discovery,' Arun said, reciting a slightly modified version of him coming to Himachal and finding my café. He omitted the part where he stalked me for days while I resisted the offer. In turn, his version sounded like the moment I knew he was a restaurateur, I had subtly but deliberately put my culinary skills on display. With a straight face, he stated how he had put me through a trial by fire to test if I could succeed at this stage, concluding that his business brain persuaded him against me, but his artistic gut had overruled that. He had weaved the account cunningly, over-crediting himself without discrediting me, so I did not mind playing along and did not refute it outright.

'You've never been to a culinary school and before Bellissimo, you never stepped inside a professional kitchen. How did you master gourmet food?' Olivia asked me.

'I always wanted to be a chef,' I said, narrating a script given by Audrey's agency. In broad strokes, the lies walked along the lines of truth but it intentionally trimmed out parts which did not make my story inspiring. The day before, there was a con-call between Ben, Arun, the agency and me to plan a strategy for this interview. Even my attire and hairstyle were predetermined. By now I was used to wearing a t-shirt and an apron in the kitchen, but for this interview I wore a traditional Indian ladies' suit with a shawl.

'It was a hot summer afternoon and this Italian couple stopped by in search of food ...' the part where I met the Italian couple was romanticised a great deal.

'As a child, I was well versed with the emotion of being hungry,' I said, amplifying our limited resources. It was not entirely untrue that we barely had enough to make ends meet, but even then, we did not know what we were missing—we were content with the mundane humility of our country life. The original draft shared by the agency hinted at portraying my father as alcoholic and against my cooking, but I had categorically rejected it.

'It is not in our hands, where our life begins, but with self-belief and perseverance, we can try taking it where we want to,' I said, ending the copy. I did believe in what I said but my conscience knew that back home, for every Sita there were a lot more Lakshmis.

'This is the most profound story I've heard in a while,' Olivia expressed, her eyes were numb. 'Sita's story is a testimony to human resilience and grit. A ray of hope for many who work hard on a daily basis to overcome the hurdles of economy, race and gender,' she narrated in her concluding remarks to the camera, painting an image of me as the poster child for female empowerment and equality, urging the youth to follow their dreams. This was my first time in front of a camera and I was not sure if I liked the pretence and the exaggeration.

'That went well,' Arun said, his car beeped. We were in the parking lot and he had come in a silver sports car, which had an unpronounceable name. Usually, a driver drove him in his black car but today he had picked me up from my home in the morning.

'Yes, but ...' I wanted to express my displeasure at the tutored script.

'I know, what we said wasn't how things happened, but remember Sita, people love to listen to what gives them hope, and hope triumphs over truth. A lot more people lie about much worse things,' he reassured. I was not sure whether he meant it or this too was a confident lie, but in spite of his self-assuming behaviour, there was always a sense of integrity to him. It sounds contradictory but that is exactly who he was.

'What is it?' he asked. I was looking at my phone.

'Nothing. My followers went from nine hundred to more than ten thousand, and they're still increasing!'

'Are you complaining?'

'It's not that ...'

'That's why we came on this show. Sita, you and your food will be known the world over,' he looked at me and said softly and then, we drove away. My inbox was overflowing. I did not have the time to read each message but people from all across the UK were writing in, mostly saying how they found my story inspirational. *Once I'm in bed, I'll reply to every single message,* I thought and kept my phone aside while my boss was driving.

'Is this the British Museum?' I asked in amazement, crossing the grey-beige coloured building with multiple pillars.

'You haven't seen much of the city?' he asked. I nodded in the negative.

'Let's take the day off,' he said.

'But ...'

'It's okay, today is anyway Gabby's brunch day,' he said and parked the car parallel to the road. He booked the tickets on his mobile; they were 'skip the queue' passes.

Inside, the expanse of the museum was breath-taking—the chequered glass ceiling cast a web of shadows beneath. We were walking through a hallway where a broken bust of an Egyptian Pharaoh stood, its eyes were so remarkably crafted, it felt like the statue was peeping into your soul. We entered the Indian section and saw multiple statues of Indian gods and goddesses in varying sizes and in different conditions, ranging from well-preserved to barely-held-together, placed in the gallery. Then there were walls, not the walls of the museum but monoliths from ancient Indian temples, which looked like they had been amputated and shipped here for display.

'All this belongs to India,' I remarked.

'These are properties of the British Museum,' asserted Arun.

'Weren't they looted during the British raj?'

'They were corroding in India, decaying to dust or demolished in wars and riots. We brought them here and conserved them for the future,' he argued.

'We? You are a Britisher?'

'British or Briton, there's nothing called a Britisher. And yes, I was born here, I am a Briton of Indian descent,' he said, softening his argumentative tone.

'All these were made in India. They represent Indian culture, history and religion. They belong in India,' I thought, not bothering to debate further. We continued with our walk and saw the entire museum. Arun's interest weaned off in the first half hour, but he kept being a patient host.

'What is it?' he probed. We were out of the museum and walking on the street. He was quite perceptive, having sensed the split second impulse I had while crossing one of the red phone booths.

'Nothing ...'

'Say it,' he said.

'It's silly.'

'Say it,' he asserted with a slight laugh.

'Don't judge. I always wanted a photo in one of these boots,' I confessed. One of our customers had gifted me a small red booth when they had come back for their second trip, ever since then I had been curious to see one for myself.

'That's it? Come,' he said and took out his phone to click my pictures. The handset inside was working! I had heard a dial tone after many years. It was one of the first working booths I had seen, the others were ransacked or turned into book shops or mobile charging spots. I took out my mobile and clicked a few selfies, then I roped in Arun. At first, he resisted, but then he gave in.

'Fish and Chips!' I screamed unintentionally while walking on the street and we stopped at a hole in the wall shop offering potato wedges and fried cod in a newspaper. I did not expect Arun to eat on the footpath, but he relished it and ordered a diet cola to accompany his meal.

'Let's go to Hyde Park,' he proposed.

We were in a slumber induced by the fried fish and potatoes and a walk in the park seemed like the right thing to do. Hyde Park was this gorgeously manicured park in the heart of the city, it was a sunny afternoon and people were out to picnic, old couples holding hands and walking, young ones sitting on the grass with their kids along with baskets full of food and a host of people lying on foldable recliners with nothing but undergarments on. Some were lying on their back and the others were prostate, like how you flip fish while it's in the pan. Most women were wearing a tiny thong with bums of various shades and sizes slow roasting in the sun.

'Don't stare,' Arun pointed out.

'Don't they have any shame?' I asked.

'Come on! Don't be one of those judgemental Indians. Have you tried it? Sunbathing?' And before I could say anything, he was already near the rental booth.

'Take a swimsuit if you like,' he offered. We were at the corner of the park, by a cylindrical shop run by an Indian man selling mobile coupons, sunscreen, umbrellas, mats, hats, sunglasses, fridge magnets, chips, beverages and bikinis. It would be hard to come up with a more random assortment.

'No, I'm fine,' I said, aghast by the thought of stripping in public.

'As you wish. I won't miss the sun for anything,' he said and casually took off his clothes and reclined on the chair, applied sunscreen on his body and wore his sunglasses. The bright sun was piercing through my shawl and I took it off. After a while, Arun stopped acknowledging my presence.

He was fit, not muscular but athletic. There was not a single hair on his body, except for his forearms and his legs. He was slothing the day away in his maroon silky underwear; I too reclined and covered my eyes with a handkerchief.

'Tea?' he asked.

He had changed back into his clothes; the sun was gone. It had suddenly become cold and windy. I had fallen asleep in the middle of a public park.

'Sure,' I said and we went to a Victorian tea house. He ordered a tea called The Pearl of Orient. I stuck to a green tea, which had a fancy name as well.

'Have you been to the West End?' he asked. 'Come, you won't regret it,' he insisted. We finished our tea and were out on the street.

'Let's walk, there's no parking there,' he suggested.

Over the next few minutes, I inhaled London, walking along the gorgeously lit and generously crowded streets at a time when the bone chilling cold had passed but the air still allowed you to relish the warm embrace of wool. Arun too was a little easy today for a man who was preoccupied on most occasions. I could hear the fleeting conversations of strangers; glancing inside overflowing pubs or just looking at people in cars and buses—we all were living in the same world yet we all had a world of our own.

'Les Miserables?' I asked; we were near the ticket counter.

'Leh Misze-rah-blah,' he said expressively and I burst out laughing.

'What are you doing?' he whispered sternly, unwilling to acknowledge the humour.

'Leh Mize-rah-blah,' I mimicked him. He was offended and walked away like a little brat; I followed. Inside the theatre, we still had to keep our masks on.

'It's a three-hour performance, don't make any noise,' he whispered and we took our seats on the balcony. The orchestra struck its first notes and the actors stepped on to the stage, then they cast on me a net woven with magic spells. I sat mesmerised by the experience, having never seen something like this before. They had pulled me into the story, on that stage, among those people, not actors but people—I shivered with every gunshot, wanted to yell with the chorus, complete their unfinished syllables and weep with every sigh. I felt their struggles, their sorrow and even celebrated with them, and every time the music would hit a crescendo, I would get goosebumps. This illusion was only broken with thunderous applause towards the end.

'What happened?' Arun asked as we were walking back to the car. It was night but the brilliantly lit street was the perfect end to the musical, like a luscious dessert sums up a meal.

'Thank you, I've never experienced something like this before,' I said softly.

'Dinner?' He asked and I nodded smilingly. We walked to Soho and found a place at a casual dining restaurant. It was bustling with people. The walls had bare bricks, the lighting and plumbing pipes were exposed and there was a live band playing, but at a volume which was not too distracting.

'Bowie once performed here,' Arun said while sipping his scotch. I smiled; I had never heard him and hoped he would not continue the conversation on this subject.

'You never thought of becoming a chef?' I asked. I caught a fleeting glimpse of regret, which was immediately concealed with a smile.

'I tried; I wasn't good. To turn your passion into a profession, you need courage and discipline; as a young man I lacked both,' he said.

'Excuse me, it's my daughter,' he said and got up to take a call. It was the first time he had mentioned his family to me—other than my brief but fateful interaction with his grandmother. I looked around, waiting for him to return. People were drinking like a lockdown was to begin.

'How old is she?' I asked when he came back.

'Ten.'

'Must be good to be ten,' I said, remembering the trauma of my mother's passing. I honestly did not know how it felt to be ten; I was ten one day and the next day, I was sixteen.

'I hope you aren't getting late.'

'I'm not, she is with her mother. I get the last weekend of the month with her,' he said. It was self-explanatory that he was divorced. Though I knew of it, I did not probe further.

'So why the food business?' I asked, wanting to know from him, what led him to give up a life of princely comforts.

'Once you find a passion, something you truly love, something you can commit to for every waking hour for the rest of your life, try as hard as you can, you can't run away from it. That's what happened to me,' Arun said.

'But you don't always need to convert your passion into a profession, right? You can just enjoy it as a hobby,' I probed his notions.

'You can, you're right. You can choose to do what you want with your passion. But the day you find your calling, the first thing you realise is how short life is,' he said deeply and paused.

'I shifted through multiple kitchen jobs in Italy before college. They were all low paying gigs and involved picking up dishes, even washing them. But during that prolonged summer, I fell in love with Italian food—their food is from the heart, with little pretence and only taste, much like Indian food,' he opened up, recounting his early adult life and how the yearning to be in the food business consumed him when he came back to finish his studies.

I had heard this story from Khan Chacha but hearing it

from Arun added a layer of warmth and passion, something I could relate to. Like him, I too tried to make other things my priority but the dam of duties I had built was not strong enough to contain the raging force of my passion for food.

'I was living a comfortable life, there was nothing I didn't have, nothing except what I really wanted to do,' he carried on.

'You should be proud of what you have achieved,' I said genuinely.

'There is a long way to go,' he said, and then was briefly lost in his own thoughts.

'Sita, the truth is, we all are failing at life—personal, professional or both. Some just aim so high that their failure lands higher than how others define success,' he added.

I had a feeling that today I had got to know more of him than I had the last six months or more.

'Isn't the idea of eating at a restaurant fascinating? Seated in the company of complete strangers, reserving a small table only to have an experience that is both—a basic necessity and a dispensable luxury—' I said, moving on to another topic to discuss.

He smiled, saying 'indeed,' and pointed his glass in the air and finished his drink.

'What's your favourite food?' I asked.

'That's a tough one, why must one choose? But the flan and the financier that Dadima makes, those are special. I'll get them for you,' he said.

We repeated our drinks; I had ordered my second gin and tonic. After that episode with the margarita, I read online about the safest drinks to order. Even though the margarita had not been the culprit, I think I will never have it again. We stuck with finger food over a heavy meal, which would have distracted from the conversation.

'What happened?' he asked. I picked up my phone out of habit and landed on Instagram. I could not believe what I saw. I had the blue tick against my name—like Hrithik Roshan!

'Nothing, I have the blue badge.'

'What's that?'

'On Instagram?'

'What does it mean?' he asked. He was surprisingly unaware about social media.

'Only famous people have it. Do you have it?'

'Neither am I on Instagram nor am I famous. I guess the two go hand in hand these days.' He paused for a moment before speaking again, 'So, should I seek an autograph,' he teased charmingly. I smiled; he slid a tissue paper and pen in front of me.

'Let me be the first to get your autograph,' he insisted, modulating his accent to make it a little more British—like Philip's; it was a bit uncharacteristic on his part, but I played along. The night felt like the last few strands of sand in the hourglass.

'Up for a drive?' He proposed while we were walking back to our car. I conceded. The car cruised carefree. We were speeding with great velocity but inside the convertible there was the serene stillness of being on a hilltop. With each passing mile, the loud and bright city was mellowing into soothing whispers and a string of festive lights. The jazz on the radio ensured the silence was comforting and not awkward.

It had been an enjoyable day, an experience I could draw no parallel to. We did nothing remarkable but it was memorable, and for the first time since coming to London, the pressure to prove myself, the resurfacing fears and anxiety were all suppressed by the sheer delight of being in the moment. Like a song coming to a conclusion, the car finally stopped under my home. Neither Arun nor I spoke, words would have only diluted the experience.

'That's it then,' he said in a deep warm tone.

'Yes, thank you,' I said shyly.

The dialogue brought us closer than we had anticipated; sports cars, after all, were not designed for two people to stay apart. He leaned forward, hesitating slightly while I stood still, then he leaned more and I pulled back a little—not drastically to retract him, but to slowly tow him through an invisible magnetic thread.

Our lips embraced and a warm shiver ran down my spine. Goosebumps! Our lips parted sooner than they touched; the insufficiency was mutual. We kissed again, slowly gaining the intensity and soon being passionately lost, a prolonged kiss with our hands on each other's back and in each other's hair. I do not know for how long we kissed, or if there were passers-by; after a point, I was sensing kaleidoscopic patterns running from my heart to my stomach. The release was natural, we did not make eye contact. I got out of the car and said a muted goodbye. I crossed the street in a hurry and unlocked the main gate in front of the stairway.

'What did I just do? Do I like him? Does he like me? Did he get carried away or was it preplanned?' I struggled with these thoughts while trying to unlock the apartment door. I took off my shoes the moment I entered the apartment. My feet were hurting! I walked towards the sink to get some water.

'Ouch!'

Something pierced my foot. It was a piece of glass, a little ahead the crystal sphere we had bought lay broken, its sparkle and glass shattered on the floor. The books and mugs from the shelf were also littered on the floor. My eyes tilted further along the ground. My heart sank and a chilling jolt ran down my spine—Baba was lying motionless on the floor.

Circle of Life

Sita

'*Baba! That's not what it's for*,' I signed after snatching the warm towel from his hands.

'Excuse me, ma'am. What would you like for lunch? Excuse me, Ma'am, lunch?' the words tore through my illusions. The adjoining chair was empty, but a coffin in the cargo carried Baba. It had been seven days since I came home to find him on the floor—it was a cardiac arrest.

Sorrow is the most bewildering of all emotions until one experiences remorse. '*I could have saved him*'. Arun and Ben stood by me while the authorities did the post-mortem. They helped me arrange a flight back. All through those days of the aftermath, I was oscillating between pain and guilt, constantly and forensically picturing the agony with which life would have left Baba. The house was a physical reminder of his striving and my failure as a daughter. He struggled from the dining table to the living room and into his room, just a couple feet short of his mobile.

'Sita, please eat something,' Ben whispered from across the aisle. He was accompanying me. I declined.

I did not know when I had fallen asleep but upon touching down and after our swab tests, we had to wait for almost four hours to receive Baba from customs.

'Madam ji, it's late, should we hold the body at the morgue for the night?' the officer at New Delhi airport asked. *My Baba was just a body now, unfit for a place among the living.* My heart and his body were decaying at the same pace.

'The hearse is here with permits, we can call it tomorrow as well,' Ben suggested.

'It's fine. We'll leave now,' I said and we were on the road by midnight, undertaking the drive to Rampur Bushahr.

'Ben, you sit with Jitender ji. I'll go with Baba,' I said. He requested that I travel in the comfort and safety of the passenger car but I did not want to leave my Baba alone—not again, never again.

'We'll follow them,' Jitender ji said.

On the highway, whenever a truck passed us, a part of me wished I would be run over, but that did not happen. If wishes were to come true, I would have never left my home.

Ben

'Jitender, do we have something to eat?' I reluctantly asked, having not eaten anything since the flight. A little while earlier we had stopped for the drivers to have their 2 a.m. tea, but Sita refused to eat and I had to give her company.

Jitender casually turned back while he was still at the wheel and handed me a polybag from the backseat. I had my heart in my mouth but was relieved to find two packets of glucose biscuits. I finished them in one go, offering Jitender a couple as well. On this trip I was further impressed with Jitender's awareness. He would routinely drive parallel to the hearse driver and check in on him, ensuring that he was not asleep and that Sita was safe. For the most part, we were just a few feet behind them. Jitender told me that the safe distance between two vehicles on a highway is when you can fully see the rear tyres of the vehicle in front, anything less and you risk a collision, anything more invites others to overtake you and wedge their motors in between. I was never a driver, earlier my finances and now my patience forbade me from driving.

Waiting for dawn, I fell asleep and when I woke up, we were at Sita's old café. The café was closed but the entire village had gathered in front. We navigated through the crowd to find a parking spot.

I saw Bittu. He was bare chested, wearing only a loincloth. With him was a middle-aged woman, a police officer and a priest; they were at the spot where we had once parked our car to convince Hira Lal and Sita to come to England.

The hearse parked first, Bittu along with his friends rushed to the car and without even meeting Sita, took the coffin out. The six men struggled to lift it, almost dropping it, and then they placed the coffin on a white cloth, right in front of the café. Two boys around twenty were trying to forcefully open it.

'Get away!' Sita blared, taking one boy by the arm and lodging him on the road.

'What's happening? Who asked you to take Baba,' she screamed at Bittu.

'Look at the tongue she's grown,' the middle-aged woman taunted. She was in a white and yellow saree with a whole lot of bangles around her wrists. She went and stood next to the police officer who had a double chin the size of a hamburger. He was breathing heavily and staring at us without blinking with his scarily big eyes.

'Bhaiya!' the old woman wailed dramatically and threw herself on the coffin.

'Let's go, I've to get back to duty,' the policeman hurriedly told the priest in his growling voice. The six men picked up the coffin and were about to proceed when Sita barricaded their advance. 'Where are you taking him?'

'For the last rites?' Bittu said unsurely.

'Leave him,' she ordered; no one complied.

'Leave!' she yelled; they put the coffin back. She broke down, hugged the coffin and cried profusely. *'Do I hug her? How will these people react?'* I thought about it as I watched the boys who were not even attempting to suppress their amusement at my appearance. Thankfully, not all who witness are blind—a couple brought a stool and a glass of water for the grieving girl. We had occupied half the highway and the honking and yelling would have brought the mountain down.

'I'm sorry for your loss beta. Pandit ji was a good man, he praised you a lot,' a man in white trousers and shirt with a gaudy watch and fake Ray-Bans, said. I could see that through the corner gap in his sunglasses, he was sneaking a peek through Sita's top.

'Beti, Negi ji was Hira's friend. He is here to help,' the policeman said. The two men then stepped back and I saw the name tag on the policeman's shirt read 'UP Sharma'. I deduced that he probably was Bittu's father and that the woman in the saree was the policeman's wife. Officer Sharma gestured towards the priest, he came forward and told Sita that it was favourable to do the last rites soon; she gathered herself and proceeded with the formalities. The casket was opened and Hira's body was placed on a ladder which was covered with a white cloth. He was then covered with flowers. The priest started murmuring some verses and the boys who had brought the coffin out of the car came forward to lift the ladder. Sita took the front spot.

'What blasphemy is this?' The middle-aged woman intercepted. 'Women can't touch the deceased,' she asserted and brought Bittu forward, urging him to take her spot.

'He is my father. I will see him off,' Sita confirmed.

'But you're not a man. Bittu was like a son to him, he will perform the last rites, only then will my brother find moksha[48],' the woman asserted.

'Pandit ji?' she instigated the priest.

'We must respect the customs, beta,' said the priest.

'If they forbid me to do my duty as a daughter, then they are not my customs,' Sita said and held her ground.

'It's okay, Pandit ji, we must change with time,' the man in the white attire came to her defence. The procession went on, I too joined the crowd, they were murmuring a chant in unison. A random man approached me and started conversing.

'Hello, Sir,' he said. I smilingly but awkwardly acknowledged him; this was no place for conversation.

'Sir, this is our son, Dipu. He also loves to cook,' the man explained. His wife and son were trotting along.

'Beta, show uncle the burger you made,' he instructed his

---

[48]Moksha: Salvation

son; the kid perhaps had no choice in the matter. I smiled but excused myself on the pretext of a phone call. When the crowd was ahead, I asked Jitender to accompany me.

'Let me get this right, women can't perform last rites?' I asked.

'No Ben ji, it's nothing like that. These priests attribute a lot to scriptures, scriptures which the common people have not read and the clergy have not understood. Our honourable Supreme Court has said women can perform last rites, but people, they would rather embrace their outdated beliefs than follow law or logic,' Jitender explained.

We arrived at the crematorium and Sita proceeded with the last rites.

Everyone came and touched Hira's feet. Sita lit the pyre. The heat made it impossible to stand in close quarters. From the narrow gaps between the wood, I could not help but catch a glance of the remains as they withered. It was unnerving to hear human bone and flesh burn to nothingness. Whether it is a hole in the ground or a heap of wood, our ultimate fate often serves as a humbling reminder to respect the gift of life.

The bystanders were now dispersing; the policeman and the man in white were the first to leave. Throughout this, Arun was messaging me, taking hourly updates on Sita's condition. As the sun set, it was only Sita, Jitender and I who were left there.

Sita

'Are you sure?' Ben asked. We had returned from the crematorium and I was busy dusting my room. Chotu had not been cleaning the house in our absence, even though he was being paid for it.

'Yes, Ben,' I declined politely; he was offering that I stay at his hotel. He asked again, but then he left. In complete solitude, I realised I was starving. I went to the kitchen. It bore a damp stench, I opened all the windows, switched on the bulb, threw away the rotting potatoes, which had gathered grey, black and green fungus. I played the 'Gayatri Mantra'[49] on my phone; it was soothing. I had reached the bottom of my ability to mourn.

I was still hungry; hunger, unlike happiness and remorse, does not pass unless you act on it. I found an unopened pack of spaghetti and there was oil, garlic and chillies, those things do not rot. I set out to make the one thing which had always comforted me.

... *'Hang in there, love,' he told his partner. Then they spoke in Italian; she was starving. His muscular forearms, with those rolled sleeves, stirred love into that pan. He took a tong to plate the spaghetti and poured warm garlic and chilli infused oil on top of it. I stood in a corner, spellbound by his wizardry. The two were sitting on a bench, holding a fork each while he held the bowl; he was barely eating—just enough to create a perception that he was so she could fill herself. They looked at me and smiled, nodded slightly, inviting me to join. I was hesitant but then I went, and he just held the bowl while I and his woman ate. I had never eaten*

---

[49]Gayatri Mantra: Indian mantra or chants for peace and wisdom

something so simple yet so divine, delicious fell short of describing it. It was hard to believe that our worn-out pan, that tea-making warhorse, was capable of stirring this symphony of flavours. At that moment I knew, that's all I ever wanted to do.

The over-boiled pasta sought my attention. The vision from all those years ago had never felt so real.

I assembled it together and started consuming it like a horse that had returned from a gallop—and what a gallop it had been! From this kitchen to that and back again, but this horse had lost her heart in the process. The pasta was enough for four, but I finished it in two minutes. I went back to my room and the sound of the crickets and the occasional howl of dogs grew louder. I lay in my bed, and felt like I had never left. I browsed through our photographs in London: Baba and I in the hotel, during our first day in the city, that impromptu trip to the Christmas market. I cherished the memory like the last piece of chocolate in a box, but then I saw our image in front of the London Eye. It was clicked right after Baba insisted that we take the ride. I broke down and howled till my throat was dry.

My uncle, his wife and Baba's sister, Saroj, the priest and Bittu were in my kitchen garden. They were talking coarsely, bringing my sleep to an unpleasant halt; it was morning already. I peeped through the window opening inwards, the man in the white attire was also with them.

'Good morning, beta,' my uncle said with a growl.

'Negi ji has arranged his car for us to immerse the mortal remains,' he said.

'Please don't embarrass me. Hira was like my brother,' Negi said. Funnily I had never seen him with Baba, but I unwillingly went ahead in his vehicle. We collected Baba's remains from the crematorium and were on the road, driving uphill to a Shiva temple on the banks of Sutlej. Negi did not come with us but he gave us his white SUV.

'Watch out, don't bang the car,' my uncle yelled from the passenger seat. Bittu was driving. My aunt and I were in the backseat with Baba's remains confined in an earthen pot, resting in my lap. Ben and the priest were cramped in the last row of this big car. Bittu was driving rashly, honking for no reason; then, his father slapped his neck, after which neither he nor the car made any unnecessary noise.

We reached the temple on the banks. The sun was shining in gentle shades of jade, here the Sutlej was still pollution-free. I dipped my feet in. The water felt like molten ice; at first the sensation was of piercing pain but soon the feet were numb, sans any feeling or pain. The priest started murmuring a prayer and I slowly surrendered my Baba's ashes to the free-flowing infinity. Then, Bittu brought out a gunny sack that had pieces of bones, bones which did not turn to ashes. I held them one by one, gently immersing them, holding on to them as long as I could; they were still warm. Each bone would bring back a smile, a moment of joy, his childish whims and his stoic self.

'Let it go, beta, only then will he attain moksha,' said the priest while I clung on to the last of what remained of my Baba; the bystanders were losing their patience. I surrendered him fully to the force of nature.

The last of his bones swirled and went to the shallow bed. I could still see it, and then, it gushed away. I kept it in sight till as far as I could, not the bone but the wave that took it.

'Let's go?' my aunt asked.

I did not respond, everyone else returned to the road. I

sat on a rock at the shallow end of the river, just a couple of feet from the bank, looking at the farthest point from where the water emerged and saw it through on the other side, to its end in sight. What I could see was not the full length of the river, it was a mere fraction of its meandering existence. But in that moment, that was the entirety of the river for me. Today, I was orphaned and alone; I was not prepared for it. I feared it and now it was upon me to bear. I took some water in my hands and drank a sip before leaving to join the others.

'Beta, what have you thought about your future?' My uncle asked as we were driving back. I was not sure what he was hinting at but he seemed to have his own plans.

'Why do you ask?' I probed.

'The foreign air has gotten to you, talking back to your elders,' my aunt taunted. I remained silent; sometimes silence is the loudest defiance.

'It's okay, she's right,' he told his wife. 'Negi ji and Hira had finalised a deal for the dhaba. It's a good price, higher than market rate. Negi ji will convert it into a modern hotel,' he expressed casually. I did not respond; he waited for a few minutes.

'I can ask Negi to give two per cent more, you will need the money for your marriage,' he said and we drove along. I checked the map on my mobile, I had to tolerate this company for another half an hour.

We reached my café, before I got down my aunt instigated me for an answer.

'I'll think about it,' I said firmly; she indeed was not pleased with the tongue I had grown.

'Don't think of me as a fool. I can see what you're up to, all this is not tolerated in our culture,' she blared on seeing

Ben get off as well. It was pointless to argue. I thanked my uncle and ignored my aunt, the moment their wheels were in motion, I was relieved. Good riddance!

'What was that all about?' Ben asked.

'Don't worry.'

'Arun has been worried. He said he wants to speak to you when you're free.'

'Thanks Ben, I'll call him.'

'Are you sure you'll sleep here?' Ben asked again. I reassured him that I was fine. Soon after, Ben left with Jitender ji.

The sun had set and a pale light lingered on, it was not soothing. Though we were well into summer, I could feel a chill deep in my bones and even my soul. Loneliness is cold and dark, the emptiness of being by myself crept on. I went into the kitchen, pushing myself to cook dinner but I did not have the will or the strength. I skipped dinner and lay in bed, surfing the internet aimlessly. Arun called, but I did not pick up. He called again. I cut his call and sent him a text, saying I wanted to be alone for now but would talk tomorrow. He replied, but I did not read the message. I switched off the lights in the room and let the sound of the river lull me to sleep.

I woke up in the middle of the night; even the crickets were asleep—it was dead silent. I could hear the breeze flute over the river in the valley. I had left the kitchen light on and was just gathering my senses to get up and switch it off. Suddenly, I heard the leaves ruffle, as if they were crushed under lurking feet. *It was not an insect—a bear? a wolf? Even worse, a man?* The sound stopped but I intuitively knew something was out there, something which did not mean well. I bolted my bedroom door and fanatically called Ben.

It was 3 a.m. I left him a text but kept on calling. With each unanswered ring, my heart paced faster. He picked up finally. I was about to speak but realised it was wise to remain silent. I saw the message tickers against—'Ben come ASAP, I'm in danger!'—turn blue; he said he was on his way.

The noise stopped but every time I convinced myself that I was imagining things, I would hear a sound in the distance, like the predator was playing hide and seek. I was afraid to breathe heavily or do anything that would give away my movements. My knees were shaking involuntarily. I heard someone descend the stairs and the door started thudding.

'Sita!' Ben yelled. I opened the door and hugged him.

'What happened?' he asked.

'Nothing, I'm scared, please sleep in Baba's room,' I requested, he willingly agreed. I went back to bed but kept the lights on. Suddenly, my phone rang—it was Bittu, he had dialled by mistake, the mobile was probably in his pocket. I heard him talk to his friend, their voices were muffled but coherent.

'I don't understand?' The friend said.

'Even I don't. Papa asked me to make noises in bushes and return,' said Bittu.

'Bhai, I confess something?'

'Yes, Bhai.'

'Your sister is very very hot. After returning from foreign, she look very hot, like models.'

'Bhai, I too have biggest confession … she is my cousin but I couldn't stop myself, I saw her display picture and …'

'Bhai! It's okay. Those people marry cousin, we can do fantasy at least,' and the boys laughed like hyenas.

'Shh …' Bittu hushed.

I cut the call. I was rotting from inside but raging at the same time.

In the morning, my aunt and the party were back in the kitchen garden. I emerged from my room and Ben from Baba's. My aunt was aghast, she was whispering something to her husband, and her expressions revealed her intentions. My uncle pressed her hand and she shut up. Negi wished me a good morning.

'What's this?' I asked, referring to the small pack his beefy bodyguard had placed in front of me.

'Payment, beta,' my uncle said with the craft of a chameleon.

'For what?'

'Beta, the deal was done by Hira,' he said, handing me a folder with stamp papers; they had my father's name and this address. At the back there was a thumb imprint over my father's name—it was fake.

'I would have signed had your son done a better job at scaring me,' I told my aunt. Their collective faces went cold like they had seen a ghost.

'You'll be off my property now. As a policeman you should know this is encroachment,' I told them.

'You slut!' my aunt snared.

'Shut up bitch. I'll claw your eyes off,' I said, prepared to turn words into action. It felt good. I had wanted to do this since she had taken away my mother's jewellery just a week after her demise.

'The papers,' Negi's stooge came forward. I tore them in front of him.

Negi fumed off without a word; he seemed vindictive. My uncle followed him; this was not over. I picked up a stick we kept in the garden to shoo the monkeys and dogs away—for my aunt it was enough; she and Bittu were on the run.

'Ben, I need a lawyer,' I told him and he was on the phone instantly.

'What happened?' Arun was on loudspeaker. We had disturbed his sleep.

'Her relatives! They're forcing her to sell the property to some goon,' Ben said loudly.

'Sita, are you all right?' Arun asked, sensing I was listening in.

'I'm fine, Arun,'

'You shouldn't stay here,' he said. 'Ben, call my uncle's lawyer, the orchard one. Leave it with me, Sita, you don't worry,' he comforted me. I agreed and I went to Ben's hotel.

'Sorry, we don't accept single ladies,' the man at the hotel reception said. Ben had a baffled expression on his face; he was not fully aware about what girls go though in India. I was thinking on my feet, and telling the receptionist that I was a local would only have made it worse.

'I am travelling here,' I said, taking out my passport and a hundred pound note I had with me. His apprehensions vapourised at the sight of foreign currency. He took the note and asked his assistant to photocopy my passport.

'No guests and visitors allowed, okay!' He had the audacity to tell me on my face. I did not bother engaging in an argument.

I checked into my room. London had spoiled me to some degree with its immaculate hotels and manicured streets. I could not help but notice the stench in the room. The bathroom was barely clean. I covered the television screen, the mirror and the key hole of the room. I was apprehensive that there may be a camera in there somewhere. I finally crashed on the bed and closed my eyes to get some peace.

We lay low for a couple of days, staying in a house arrest within this hotel. It felt like the time when Lakshmi's body had been found and every girl in the village grew afraid to step out. Finally, we got a call from the local police station and I was back at my café.

'Sharma ji, it is your responsibility that no one troubles her, otherwise there is trouble for you,' the young IPS officer threatened my uncle. She was thirty at best, but the authority she wielded was intimidating for anyone who dared to disobey her.

'And you, mind your own business. You don't want us to look deeper into what you do,' she warned Negi. My uncle and Negi nodded obediently, but on the inside, they were shivering like lambs caught in the rain.

'If someone troubles you, call my mobile,' the young IPS officer shook my hands and said. She was the top cop in the area. One visit from her had put an end to my woes. Arun's grandmother was from Himachal and her family was well connected here, that is why a cop of her rank had personally looked into the matter. Arun did not tell me that he had done anything, but I knew he was behind this.

'Come?' asked Ben.

'Thanks Ben, but I'll stay here now,' he understood and gave me a hug before leaving.

I sat in the café; the silence was comforting but the void of loneliness had not eased. It had been an emotional rollercoaster; the hovering vultures I once called family, had robbed me of my ability to mourn peacefully.

'Hello, Didi,' I heard a familiar voice from behind me. It was Chotu. For the past week, whenever I thought of him, it was with a slight bit of annoyance for all the work he had not done in our absence but now, upon seeing him, I could not help but smile and give him the cap I had bought for him from London. His happiness was beyond measure. I picked up a carton and signalled at him to join in on the cleaning; he was on it. We worked vigorously for a couple of hours.

Cleaning the café meticulously, visiting every square inch of its interiors set me to wonder—my life was now in London, without Baba what would I do with this house and the café? Perhaps it was best I sold it. If not to that slime Negi, then to someone who was willing to have a fair deal and pay a good price.

Seeing the café open, a car stopped at the threshold and two children and a couple got out. At first, I thought of telling them that we were shut, but then I decided against it. Their arrival made me feel like when I had welcomed the customers the first time I opened my café. They took a seat and I went to take their order and explained that we haven't fully opened. I served them tea and biscuits. Seeing them smile, being lost in their conversations, I realised how much I missed my own café, a place I had built myself.

The money they paid, I gave to Chotu. He was delighted.

My phone was buzzing, it was Arun. He asked how I was and made no mention of the lawyer or the police officer he had arranged. I thanked him nonetheless.

'What's the plan now?' he asked.

'I'll sell the place and return.'

'Ben and the lawyer will help you with that,' he said. I asked how he was and how the restaurant was doing. The conversation was a little awkward after what happened when we last saw each other; I hoped things would naturally settle when I returned. There were some questions I had to answer about my feelings for him.

'Didi, what do we do with this?' Chotu asked, he was holding an old tin board kept under the counter. It read 'Pandit ji ki Tapri' in Hindi, the original board of Baba's tea stall before I had revamped it. I held the dented and dusty signage. It was like a screen playing a montage of memories. Arun was still on the call, but I was not ...

'What's wrong with this?' Baba expressed his resistance when he realised how much the new board would cost.

'We need to be modern, Baba. We need to attract those families and tourists, these truck drivers won't eat what I want to make,' I argued, my hands moving assertively while conveying this to him. 'Plus, they'll pay a lot more,' I signed softly. He was not convinced but he agreed to change the name and fund the makeover of his stall, which I was soon to take over.

'Sita, are you there?' I heard the voice faintly on my handset. Arun was yelling from the other side.

'Arun, I'll speak with you later. Bye,' I said and hung up. I took a dust cloth and started cleaning the board.

Ben

'What do you mean you can't convince her!' Arun was yelling at me from the other side. Over the past two days, I was busy helping advocate Ranaut find the right client for Sita's property. When I reached her café, I did not expect to see what I saw.

'I don't know, Arun, the café is up and running,' I said; he did not listen and continued to blare. 'Let me talk to her again,' I said apologetically. He hung up.

Sita was busy talking to the local women from the area and a part of the café had a tiny make-do training station. The board at the entrance had changed. It wasn't that petite signage of 'The Midway Café,' which had attracted us but an old tin board with something written in Hindi. Hira Lal and a woman's photograph were on a wall.

'Hi Ben. Can you please pass those utensils?' Sita told me. She was taking a cooking class for these women!

'Sita, we have found a buyer, they are coming in an hour to see the place,' advocate Ranaut said but she was invested in teaching the women how to cook pasta sauce.

'Ranaut ji, you'll have to ask them to cancel,' she said softly. The lawyer was confused, I pitied him. Arun had stalled him on our last trip and now Sita did.

'What happened, Sita?' I inquired.

'Ben, I can't thank you enough,' she held my hands and said. 'But I have to be here,' she pressed my hands.

'You're coming with me, aren't you?' I asked. Our flight was scheduled for tomorrow. She shook her head in disagreement.

'But ... you will come back, right?' I asked to find some consolation but she did not respond.

'You've worked so hard, don't throw it all away,' I pleaded.

'I had thrown it all away Ben. I am just trying to reclaim the memories now.'

'And Arun? He'll never agree. You'll have to call him and explain,' I asked.

'It's not his decision to make Ben,' she said.

I was a little surprised but I did not judge her decision.

'*Even the most magnificent sculpture would prefer the obscure comfort it once had in the heart of a mountain,*' I thought. We had taken her out of her home and given her the world, but for her, her world was always here with her father.

'Think it over, Sita, not many can achieve what you have in such a short span,' I said and she just placed her hand on my cheek.

'Thank you, Ben,' she expressed and we hugged tightly. I had a looming premonition that this was probably the last time I was going to see her, at least for a while.

'Thank you, Ben,' she said again as I sat in the car.

Our eyes were numb, I reached out from the window and squeezed her hand tightly. I do not remember the last time I cared so deeply about someone.

'Let's go, Jitender.' The wheels were in motion, it had truly been a long haul.

❀

Sita

Even though I knew he would come, I was still shocked to see him. It had been a week since Ben had left and I had stayed back. And now, on a sunny summer afternoon, Arun was standing at my threshold.

I gestured at him to take a seat. With a bittersweet flashback, I recollected the times when he would visit on a daily basis to persuade me to come to London.

'You didn't need to come,' I said. Over the past week I had ignored his calls, then Ben called and Arun took the line. We spoke briefly and upon hearing of my desire to stay back, he didn't argue further.

At that moment I knew—he was coming.

'I wouldn't have, had you ...' he said warmly. I asked Chotu to make two cups of tea and when he returned with the cups, I signalled for him to leave us alone. I should have been happy to see Arun, on a personal level, perhaps I was, but I had also been dreading the game of persuasion he had already begun.

'You've restarted the café?' he asked and I nodded.

'And what do you plan to do with it?' he probed.

'What I had been doing all this while. And I'll teach more women,' I told him. I had renamed the café back to its original identity and along with serving the travellers, I started teaching the basics of professional cooking to the women of our village. This would help them earn a living and allow me to fuel my creativity and scale-up into catering and pre-packed food. I wasn't sure if this was a good idea or if this would be successful, but this is what I wanted to do.

'You know, all this can continue to run in your absence. You can pay an annual visit and we can hire a manager. This lad, Chotu, seems reliable too,' Arun explained. I was listening without responding.

'Take a break, a month? All of summer if you need to,' he coaxed.

'I don't know, Arun. This is what I must do and this is where I must be,' I asserted.

'You can't be serious, Sita. It's career suicide, you are wasting your talent here,' he argued.

'No, Arun. I have chosen peace over glory.'

'I'm staying here too,' he rattled like a little boy.

'Please don't, I am not coming back,' I said conclusively; this argument went on for a while, acquiring new words each time.

'I won't force you to do anything, Sita, just know that Bellissimo will always be your restaurant to come back to,' he said helplessly.

'Arun, thank you. I know I'll see you again, it won't be now though,' I said and we shared a moment of silence. In our heads we probably recollected the same images: meeting each other for the first time, him fanatically trying to convince me to come to London, the day when he threw the garlic on the wall, the time when he drunk-walked through the kitchen, the contest, our time at the museum, the drive ... and the kiss. The memories brought a droplet of fondness in my eyes, but I had to resist the temptation.

'We didn't drink the tea,' he held my hands and said. We both laughed, and like a vine intertwines with a trellis, we embraced. It was a prolonged hug. At first, I was conscious whether there were any passers-by, but the warmth I found in his arms evaporated those concerns. I wanted to kiss him. I really wanted to and maybe he thought of it too, but none of us made a move.

'You must leave now,' those weren't the words I wanted to say.

He agreed, perhaps unwillingly, but without any resistance; his eyes had the sheen of dewdrops. I came to the threshold to see him off. He opened the door of the car but he paced back to hug me again.

'Promise me, I'll see you again.'

'You will, Arun, I promise,' I said and we both melted into a warm kiss, never did separation feel so comforting. He was conscious that it was not London and I still had to live here. We left our embrace like how two pages stuck with glue are separated from each other.

He sat in the car and was looking at me through the glass in the back; I saw his car turn around the curve, watched until a trail of dust was left behind. Bidding adieu to the dead seems difficult until you have to do it with the ones who are still alive.

I returned to the café and put another cup of tea to brew, the same ginger-cardamom tea Baba used to make. It was 3.15 p.m. I had a golden hour before the tea-seekers would come. I poured the tea into a tiny glass, turned on the radio and tuned it to catch the signal. I came back to the window overlooking the valley and took a sip which transported me back to the same place ...

It was late summer afternoon, the gravel on the road was being laid by a road roller to widen the lane. The dust and the noise tore through the tranquillity of the valley. Baba's hair was still black, he was upstairs at the tea stall, brewing tea for truckers.

'Sita come,' Ma called. She was frying pakoras in the kitchen downstairs. I was seven and blissfully swinging on a tyre hung by a rope in our lawn; it was not a kitchen garden then, just a dusty playground of my childhood. Ma was wearing a green saree and smiling at me, I felt like a flower and she, my soil. Baba came down. I did not hear him; he was masterful at concealing his steps. He picked me up in his arms, I was suspended horizontally in his armpit, laughing and resisting this ticklish abduction. We sat outside our humble home. Baba tuned the transistor, he could not hear anything but looked at Ma to confirm that the signal was received, a Hrithik Roshan song was playing on the local station. We sat there, the three of us, laughing and eating the pakoras

and sipping the sweet ginger tea. I carried on with my mischief, running around the lawn; Baba extended his arm and caught me. Ma's hand caressingly ran through my hair, her lips pressed against my cheeks. Baba hugged me, Ma joined in and I embraced them tightly, our laughter echoed through the valley.

I was home and I was happy.

Acknowledgements

I thank with deepest gratitude:
  Chef Thomas Zacharias
  Chef Ruchira Hoon, The Ruchira Kitchen
  Chef Aditi Goel, Sakara Hospitality
  Chef Radhicka Agarwaal, The Daily Gourmet
  And Rahul Bakshi, Marriott International
  For their inputs on the nuances of the culinary and hospitality elements depicted in this book. I also appreciate the invaluable support Mita Kapur at Siyahi extended for this story.

  Lastly, I am thankful to Aishwarya Lahiri for being my sounding board during the editing of this book.